IN THE DIRT

A Baseball Detective Story

By

John M. Mulligan

Cover design by: Samantha Ewert

This book is dedicated to everyone who ever coached the game of baseball at any level, in recognition of the pain and joy involved in teaching the game.

PROLOGUE

October 1994

Canaugh made coffee and toast in his apartment. He liked to get up just before sunrise each day because the breakfast nook in his apartment was its only nice feature. It had a large window facing east, which gave him a view of the mountains from the second floor. Almost all apartments in Santa Fe were limited to two floors to maintain the historic appearance of the small city. All buildings in Santa Fe were limited in height. Their color palette, due to a local ordinance, ranged only from beige to shades of brown. Canaugh had decided that the low buildings and monotone earth colors of the city gave him the sense of calm that he needed. Even though he considered himself to be a man in hiding, he liked to walk the streets in daylight hours. He'd go to Mass many mornings at Saint Francis Cathedral. He'd sit in the back and watch. He chose the back in the hope that he could avoid shaking hands with anyone during the handshake ritual of the Mass. Though he considered himself a Catholic, he hadn't gone to church many Sundays in his life due to having played baseball, and then due to his work as a cop and a private investigator. Going to church helped give him some peace of mind. Santa Fe was so different from anyplace else he'd been in the U.S., and especially different than anyplace in Minnesota, where he'd spent most of his life.

Hearing the paper carrier's steps to his front door every morning was a reliable wake-up call to Canaugh. Despite the weeks that had gone by since he'd left Minneapolis, the sound of footsteps on the outside stairway any time of day or night caused him to become alert. He would consciously measure his proximity to his loaded service revolver, retained from his days as a Minneapolis cop, which he kept in the bedroom closet. The paper carrier for the Albuquerque Journal was not some freckle-faced kid, like the paperboy who delivered the St. Cloud Times to his parents' home in Albany many years ago. She was Hispanic, fortyish, slim, and pretty. She came the same time every morning. From time to time, if Canaugh was dressed, he would open the door and exchange an "Hola" with her, and she would give him the smallest of shy smiles.

Canaugh took his time each morning reading the sports pages, noticing the gradual change in light from the desert's purplish dawn to another sunny New Mexico day. Canaugh set down his paper and looked out at the shadows sliding down the distant mountains as the sun rose in the sky.

Canaugh took stock of his situation. He was in one of the most beautiful places he'd ever seen. He had just enough money to live on. He missed seeing his friends in Minnesota, but not so much that he was willing to risk his life to go back there, or to disclose to them where he was. He purposely didn't have much human contact where he lived now, other than to occasionally introduce himself by using his phony made-up name.

He remembered from his minor league baseball days sharing an apartment one summer in a small Southern town with another pitcher who had successfully romanced away the girlfriend of one of the local greasers. Aware that he could be the target of a jealous man, the pitcher made a practice of setting out glass Pepsi bottles behind the apartment door each night. Canaugh had thought the practice was dumb and he told his roommate so.

It was 9:00. Canaugh put on his jacket and took a stroll. When he walked past the Safeway, he stopped in and bought a six-pack of Pepsi in glass bottles. Back in his apartment, he wondered whether to drink the Pepsi or pour it down the drain. He had no appetite for Pepsi at his age, but he was too frugal to just throw it away.

Canaugh sat in his apartment without turning on the lights or the radio, enjoying the silence. For the first time ever, despite having been a cop and then a private investigator, he was afraid for his life. He sipped his Pepsi from the bottle while he thought of all the chapters of his life. *How did this happen?* he said to himself.

BOOK I

CHAPTER 1

May 1948

Vince Canaugh walked warily to the mound at the home field of the Albany, Minnesota Huskies. In baseball, the infielders and outfielders usually run in small clusters onto the field to start an inning, but a pitcher walks alone. It was the top of the seventh and final inning, and the Huskies had a 5-0 lead over the visiting team from Melrose High School. More important than the score, to Canaugh at least, was that the Melrose Dutchmen had no hits, and that Canaugh was three outs away from his second no-hitter of the season and the fourth no-hitter of his high school career. Canaugh was a slim left-hander, six feet two inches tall with reddish-blonde hair and uncommonly light blue eyes. It was rare to have a hot day for a game in Minnesota high school baseball. The season started the second week of April when the ice had just barely melted out of the lakes in central Minnesota. Often in the early season games it was so cold that players wore long johns under their uniforms. Pitchers got into the habit of blowing into the fist of their throwing hand between pitches to keep it warm enough to grip the baseball.

Today was unseasonably warm, so warm that just before the game started Canaugh slipped behind the small concrete block restrooms and took off his long sleeve pitcher's undershirt.

The Huskies, like most Minnesota high schools, used wool flannel uniforms owing to baseball tradition and mostly to the fact that no one had come up with a durable alternative to flannel. Flannel uniforms held their shape well, didn't wrinkle, and didn't tear when players slid into base. Canaugh was grateful most of the season for the warmth that wool flannel provided. Today, he realized, the back of his jersey was already soaked with sweat from his pre-game warm-up.

Canaugh threw his warm-up pitches before the final inning. He no longer had a concern that Albany would win the game over Melrose. He knew that sitting on the six rows of splintery bleachers behind home plate were not only Joe Purvis, the sports columnist from the St. Cloud Times, but also two men who were baseball scouts for professional baseball teams. Jarvis Anderson, the Albany coach (and math teacher), told Canaugh as he was warming up in the outfield before the game that the scouts for the Washington Senators and the St. Louis Cardinals had just introduced themselves, and each had a few questions for him about Canaugh. The scout for the Senators looked familiar to both Canaugh and to Coach Anderson, and the coach told Canaugh that he was pretty sure that he had seen the guy before at previous games. The scouts, in sunglasses, wore straw hats along with short sleeve dress shirts and narrow black ties, unusual apparel at baseball games in Minnesota's small towns.

The first batter for Melrose took his stance with his toes across what remained of the chalk line that marked the batters' box. Canaugh could see that the batter was crowding the plate, either hoping to get hit by a pitch or to rattle Canaugh. Canaugh's instinct was to throw inside and high to brush the batter back and show the batter that he didn't appreciate where the batter had taken his stance. As Canaugh started his wind-up, the batter leaned in further, so that Canaugh's pitch coming inside hit the batter on the chest with a glancing blow. Though the batter made no effort to avoid the pitch, as baseball rules required, the umpire signaled that the batter could take first base. Canaugh stared with dismay at the ump because the ump should have called the batter out. Adding to Canaugh's annoyance, Schouweiler, the catcher, called time and came trotting to the mound to talk to Canaugh. If the scouts had not been in attendance, Canaugh likely wouldn't have cared, but Canaugh was concerned that the scouts might have thought he had control problems. Schouweiler was a capable catcher, but he liked to sweat over small details. "You OK?" asked Schouweiler. Canaugh just gave him a look that he hoped would send Schouweiler back behind the plate without his having to say a word. "Shake it off," said Schouweiler as he turned and headed back to the plate.

The next Melrose batter also took up his stance close to the plate, toes out of the box, though he lined up on the left side of the plate. Too close, thought Canaugh. It irked him when players didn't follow the rules of baseball. He realized that two batters in a row doing the same thing meant that they were taking instructions from Melrose's coach. The Melrose coach knew what Canaugh had learned in his years of playing varsity baseball, though his own coach had never spoken of it. Small town Minnesota baseball often meant only one ump, who worked behind the plate and could sometimes see the plays on the basepaths, and sometimes not. And when they couldn't see, they made guesses at what had happened.

It was hard to find umpires in the small towns northwest of St. Cloud, and so athletic directors settled for what they could find among the willing. What could be found among those willing to take two-hour umpiring jobs on weekday afternoons were mostly those who didn't have jobs of any kind. The small pay they got went to buy the week's groceries or liquor. Some umps were retired guys with gray hair, whose vision and hearing were suspect. Some umps, Canaugh figured, got the job only because they owned a mask, a chest protector, and a whisk broom. From his pitching experience Canaugh knew that there was no uniformity in strike zones, and part of his task was to figure out what the ump of the day would consider the strike zone. Being a pitcher meant figuring out things that no one, not the coach or any of his teammates on the field, could help him with. One thing Canaugh had finally figured out as he ended his high school days was to control his temper and not argue or challenge an umpire. The umps he'd dealt with may not have been all that knowledgeable about baseball rules. They may not have been highly able to see everything that they needed to, but they did know that they had authority to stifle any wise-ass high school ballplayer. None of them were going to take crap as part of earning their twelve dollars for the afternoon's work.

For the next batter, Canaugh shook off the sign because he had something in mind. His first pitch was a fastball, as hard as he could throw it, that was intentionally outside. Canaugh wanted the batter to see how fast he could throw the ball so that a batter deciding to get hit by a pitch would have his courage tested. The pitch hit the catcher's mitt with a pop as loud as a firecracker and Canaugh thought he saw a bit of fear on the batter's face. For his second pitch, Canaugh got the sign he wanted and threw his best curve which was intentionally aimed high. The batter saw the pitch headed straight for his head and jumped out of the way just as the ball dropped and curved across the plate for strike one. Canaugh got the sign for another curve and threw the same pitch. The batter didn't jump out of the box this time, but leaned way back so that he wasn't ready to swing when the ball curved and dropped across the plate. Ahead in the count, Canaugh threw a fastball outside which the batter took a weak swing at, anxious to end his at-bat without injury or further embarrassment.

With one out, Canaugh figured that the runner on first would get the sign to steal so that the Dutchmen would have a runner in scoring position. Canaugh had an excellent pick-off move, which he had polished in his three years pitching for the varsity. By just delaying a fraction of a second on his usual stretch motion, he caught the runner leaning into his planned break to second, and the runner was picked off. Suddenly there were two outs, and Melrose's plan to get at least one run seemed deflated. Canaugh checked the scouts in the stands and was pleased to see that they were both making a note on their clipboards. The last batter for Melrose knew the game was lost, and that he was no match for Canaugh. He was out on three straight strikes.

After the game, the scouts took turns shaking hands with Canaugh and introducing themselves. They had business cards with their team logos printed in color on them. They asked for and got the home phone number and mail address for the Canaugh residence. They asked the coach if he had the summer schedule for the Albany American Legion team. Canaugh's teammates lingered at a distance, excited to see major league scouts talking to one of their players, before they headed to the locker room for showers.

As the afternoon turned to evening, Canaugh walked home alone from the high school. Tulips and lilacs, Minnesota's floral emblems of spring, were blooming in the gardens of the smallish homes in Albany. He was excited. He'd gotten two no-hitters for the season and another win pitching for the Huskies. Graduation was in less than ten days and then his high school days were over. He'd been admitted to St. Cloud State. He'd applied because he was unsure how his senior season would work out, and mostly because his mother insisted. He felt that afternoon, for the first time, that he had a future playing baseball, something he'd hoped for. If any team made an offer to sign him, no matter how little money was on the table, he'd take it. *The best day of my life*, he thought as he approached the family home on a shady street.

CHAPTER 2

March 1948

Vince Canaugh was an only child. Being an only child in the heavily Catholic St. Cloud area in the fifties and sixties made Canaugh a rarity. The bishops and priests in the St. Cloud diocese preached from the pulpit that the purpose of marriage was to have children. The Catholics of Stearns County dutifully responded by having large families. Many of Canaugh's friends came from families of six or more children. There were two families in Albany with twelve children. Canaugh never knew why his parents only had one child. It was a topic he never was going to ask his parents about, and it was certainly a subject they were not going to bring up. He had no way of knowing whether it was a choice his parents had made, or if either one of them had a physical problem. In Albany, his mother was at a disadvantage when other families came to St. Anthony's Church with numerous children trailing behind their parents, in descending sizes like a set of front porch steps. When he got older, Canaugh thought he detected a quiet sadness in his mother when other families celebrated one after another their children's Holy Communion or high school graduation.

Canaugh's father Andy called himself a home improvement contractor, though others called him a handyman. He used his skills to do carpentry and concrete work when people in town made repairs or even small incremental improvements to their homes in the post-War era. He also took on jobs that required lesser skills such as painting, wallpapering, and putting on storm windows for widows. If more successful contractors and home builders in town had more work than they could handle, they would call on him to supplement their own crews. Most of the time the work was steady, for he had a reputation as a sober church-going family man, even if not particularly skilled, and that was enough to get him steady work.

Andy's income was sufficient to support the little family of three, though, like most of the families in Albany at that time, they were careful with their money. They always bought used cars. They got maximum life out of the clothes they bought at J.C. Penney's in downtown St. Cloud. Canaugh's mother Eunice clipped newspaper coupons from the grocery store for her shopping. ("That way the paper pays for itself" she would often say.) Upon her return from the store, she would paste the S&H Green Stamps given to her at check-out in the coupon books she kept in a kitchen drawer. Canaugh had no memory of the stamp booklets ever being redeemed for anything. When Canaugh started seventh grade, Eunice took a job at the Federated Store in Albany selling fabrics and patterns. She liked fabrics and she liked even more talking about fabrics, sewing, and the latest developments in Albany with her customers. Working at Federated was considered respectable employment for women in Albany.

The Canaughs lived in a three-bedroom house on Baldwin Avenue, built in the 1920's. It had white clapboard siding and green imitation shutters (the shutters were wooden, but only decorative because they were attached to the house and didn't close.) On the south and west sides of the house there were striped aluminum awnings over the windows, as was commonly done in Albany. Metal awnings weren't particularly attractive but having them over the windows protected the furniture inside from being faded by the sun, even though it made the house interior a bit dark. The house was small, but its compact size made little difference because it was on a street of small homes. The house was close to the sidewalk, so the front yard had only room for lilac bushes and a concrete birdbath that Eunice favored. The back yard was much more spacious. It had room for Vince and his father to play catch most evenings, except when his father came home too tired from the day's labors. Realizing that Vince's zest for playing catch greatly exceeded his own, Andy splurged on a pitching frame at Sears. It had a honeycomb string net edged by metal springs. Woven into the net was a nylon ribbon which marked the strike zone. The device was advertised that pitches would bounce back to the thrower, but this worked more in theory than in practice. Some pitches came back to Vince all right, but many caromed off in unexpected angles so that Vince had to hustle to field them. Vince set up the frame against the side of their detached one-stall garage. The garage had been painted more recently than the house, so it had a noticeably different hue of whiteness. The frame was not large (the larger size cost more than Andy cared to pay) so when Vince spent his afternoons throwing balls to the frame, the ball would occasionally miss and hit the garage with a sound like a gunshot. His mother had brittle nerves. If she was home, she would after a while stick her head out the door and tell Vince not to make so much noise. He learned to concentrate on the frame and gradually hit the net with every pitch.

When Vince reached high school age, he had gotten taller. The strength in his left arm and his ability to keep the ball over the plate got noticed by the baseball coach. The coach first used Vince, only a freshman, as a reliever but by his sophomore year he was a starter and becoming known in the area for his pitching ability. In high school, he made the Honor Roll. Though not at the top of his class, he was acknowledged by the teachers and his fellow students as being clever and always prepared. He stood out among his classmates for reading lots of books, astonishing his classmates by doing reading that wasn't assigned.

The girls in high school perceived Vince as friendly. Not all of them were enamored of his red hair, but they were all aware of his striking ice-blue eyes. Like many of his guy classmates, Vince wasn't yet comfortable talking to girls and not very assertive in making his feelings known. Girls were puzzled that he wasn't asking any of them out on dates. After Thanksgiving in his senior year, Vince began eating school lunch a couple times a week with Carol Chestnut. Carol was the best student in the class and perceived by her classmates as headed for bigger things. She was wholesome in appearance, though not viewed as particularly attractive by the guys because she wore her hair in a short and prim style. She wore little make-up, only a pinkish lipstick. Her wardrobe tastes tended towards the conservative and modest. She favored plaid skirts, well over the knee, and drab Scandinavian sweaters, worn large and bulky, and not tight over her bosom like the girls that the guys noticed and admired.

What mystified the students about the apparently growing relationship between the two was that Carol was the daughter of the Lutheran minister. In Albany, Catholics and Lutherans were discouraged from dating each other by their respective churches and by some unspoken rules best described as "community understanding". The Lutheran minister was the Reverend Elwood Chestnut. About half a dozen of the town's most successful businessmen took the liberty of calling him "Woody", but to everyone else of all faiths he was known only as "Reverend Chestnut." Reverend Chestnut's sermons tended to speak in absolutes, with little regard for subtlety. He had a bulldog's build and a florid, somewhat unfriendly face. He was a forceful speaker with strong opinions about morality. He was held in high regard by those in his congregation. As time went by, Canaugh would walk Carol home after school, though by agreement they would stop and separate two blocks from the church parsonage. "We're just friends" they would say to their skeptical peers and their parents when asked, and they got asked often.

At Albany High School the big mid-winter dance was called The Snow Ball. It was the high school's counterpart to the Homecoming Dance held in the fall. For each of them, a teen band would be hired from St. Cloud and students wore their best attire. Carol arranged to go with two of her friends. Vince went by himself, though he secured the use of the family car by fibbing to his parents that he had a date. Vince spent part of the afternoon clearing the car of his father's tools and paint cans. At the dance, he stood in the shadows, talking to guys. He did dance slow numbers when a couple of the girls who had come without dates asked him to dance. After almost two hours, with mutual nods to each other, he and Carol shared a dance. Carol pressed her cheek next to his and held him tightly. Vince was aware that many people were watching this display, and he thought he saw both smirks and guys elbowing each other in the ribs. After the one dance they parted, with Carol hanging onto his hand longer than necessary before they parted.

Vince left the dance and waited in the car, warming it up. He was joined in a few minutes by Carol who said, somewhat naively, that she was sure no one saw her leave. She slid over next to Vince and held his gloved hand with her gloved hand. Vince headed out to a country road he'd picked out and stopped the car. On Minnesota winter nights, teens know that it's necessary to leave the car running with the heater on if their interlude was going to take more than a few minutes. The couple kissed passionately for the first time. They made out with great vigor, though neither had much experience in this endeavor. After a while, she unbuttoned her coat, and Vince cupped her breast with his left hand. She gasped in his ear but made no effort to resist. Vince had never been this close to Carol, or for that matter any girl, and so he was taken by the aroma of her lipstick, her perfume, and her hair spray. From their friends they had heard about the importance of not leaving any marks on the skin, so they used care. After half an hour, Carol said to Vince, punctuated by short kisses, "I need to get home." Carol checked her watch. She knew that she needed to be going through her front door within 20 minutes after the ending time of the dance. Her parents would be awake, though hopefully not in the living room. The couple sat far apart for the ride back into town and down the main street. Vince let her off at their usual parting spot, two blocks from the parsonage. She got out of the car and winked at Vince and said, "Wish me luck." Carol braced herself to lie to her parents, if necessary. A forbidden romance seemed exciting to her.

Vince drove home with the windows of the car open, hoping that the fresh air, though frigid, would clear all of Carol's feminine aromas from the family car. The house was dark. His parents had gone to bed. He undressed and got into bed. He decided that he was in love and that Carol was the perfect girlfriend for him. He certainly liked the feeling of her mouth on his, and their long, deep kisses. Perhaps they had a future together. As for the disapproval of both parents to this arrangement, they would have to somehow deal with it, though he didn't know how. All he knew was that he liked how he felt.

By Monday, Vince and Carol were back to their school routine. Not much was made of their very public dance and apparently no one had seen them disappear from the dance at about the same time or seen them driving back into town after their passionate session on the back roads outside of town. In their classes together or when passing in the halls they would exchange meaningful glances. On one of their walks home, Vince asked about seeing her again, possibly a regular form of date. Carol reported to Vince that her parents were suspicious, and that would have to wait. Once, after a trip to the mall in St. Cloud, Carol gave Vince a paperback copy of "Romeo and Juliet" that she bought at B. Dalton.

The beginning of spring, for high school seniors planning on going to college, meant looking for and receiving college acceptances, followed by a business-like exchange of letters in the mail about dorm assignments and freshman orientation. Carol was going to Valparaiso in Indiana, on full scholarship; a Lutheran college that ensured the offspring of financially struggling Lutheran ministers were taken care of. In her conversations, she began referring to her destination as "Valpo" which, after a while, Vince found annoying.

One day while walking her home, Vince asked Carol to the Prom, which was scheduled for mid-May. In Minnesota high schools, the Prom for many is a ritual for couples declaring the seriousness of their relationship. It's rarely a first date for the participants. Neither Vince nor Carol had been to the Prom as juniors. In response to the invitation, Carol seemed grateful and happy, though all sorts of emotions showed on her face. Two days later, over a school lunch of chicken a la king, Carol brought up the subject of Prom. Her face was solemn, and she was quickly on the verge of tears. "We can't go," she said. "I'm too afraid to bring it up to my parents. It's mostly my father; he wouldn't approve. I'm sorry, I want to go with you, but I can't." She placed her hand on his as she added, "I hope you understand."

Vince was suddenly aware of other students staring at the two of them. Vince felt miserable. He withdrew his hand from under hers, mainly out of embarrassment, and was silent for a long time. "It's OK," he said. "We can work something out." He had no idea of what could be worked out. They ate the rest of their lunch in silence.

Another couple of weeks went by, with Vince and Carol eating lunch off by themselves several days a week. Vince no longer walked her home after school because he had baseball games or practice right after school. One day at lunch, Carol asked Vince to meet him outside on the lawn when lunch was finished. It was a warm spring day and there were several students sitting on the grass for the rest of their lunch hour. They found a shady corner of the school's front lawn and sat down. Carol had a wary look when she told Vince that she was going to the Prom with Art Huebner.

"Art Huebner?" Vince asked in surprise, and more than a little pain, because Art was a bit overweight, didn't play sports, and was widely regarded as lacking in social graces. "He's a dork."

Carol got defensive. "He's all right. His family goes to our church. He's going to Luther in Decorah next fall and my father likes him. Besides, I've never been to a Prom and this is my last chance."

Vince felt the pain of picturing the girl he ached for in the sweaty embrace of a guy he disliked. He also felt the pain of embarrassment that would accompany the news around Albany High. The girl known as his not-so-secret girlfriend was going to the Prom with a flabby guy with low social status in the school. He felt anger and mortification at the same time, but he remembered all that he'd learned playing baseball about self-control. After a long pause, he said quietly, "I'm glad I heard it from you."

Vince considered going to the Prom with some other girl, but that didn't feel right to him. He spent Prom night at home reading a book about baseball. He concentrated on playing baseball and having a good senior season. The cafeteria lunches with Carol stopped. The long serious looks between them in class and the hallways did not. He called her house once and left a message with her mother, but the call never got returned. What Vince needed, though it was hard for him to figure out, was some finality to his relationship with Carol. It wasn't coming.

CHAPTER 3

Winter of 1949-50

Once he graduated from high school, Canaugh spent the summer with the Peninsula Pilots, a rookie league team in Hampton, Virginia. He'd signed a minor league contract for a $2,000 bonus. Canaugh gave most of the money to his parents because they needed a better car. He'd made no plans for the off-season, so he'd returned to home in Albany. The minor league baseball season was done by Labor Day because in the small cities and towns across America where the lower minor league teams played it was difficult to sell tickets after that holiday. It was generally understood by the population that, regardless of the weather in any state, summer was over on Labor Day and then it was football season at that point. Home was different after being gone. While his parents had been sad to see him leave home after graduation, he had the feeling that they were a bit sad to have him back home. His good high school friends were off in college, and while some came home on weekends, he saw very little of them. He didn't feel right trying to date girls still in high school, even though they were almost his age. There was no one to do things with. He could stay in shape because he was still welcome at the high school gym after school. While the boys' basketball team practiced, he ran laps and played catch with Crandall, whom he did not know well, but would be the starting catcher for the baseball team in the spring season. Restless and bored, he found a job at the lumberyard loading and unloading trucks. The job was boring, and being outdoors all day was chilling, but he justified it on the basis that it paid fairly well for a small-town job and helped keep him in shape.

After his second season spent with the Greenville Spinners, Canaugh had made arrangements to start college as a freshman. The Minnesota state college system operated on the Quarter system. Fall Quarter started the last week of September and ended just before Christmas. Winter Quarter started right after New Year's Day and finished in mid-March. Canaugh had realized (actually his mother was the one who realized it and communicated it to him repeatedly) that he could attend St. Cloud State for Fall and Winter Quarters. Going to college for Spring Quarter was out of the question due to baseball season starting well before the Quarter was finished. Canaugh and his parents came to an agreement that they would pay half the cost of his attending college if he would pay the other half. Neither Canaugh nor his parents could afford college without making some sacrifices. Canaugh knew that he would have to get a job on campus to pay for his half share because playing baseball in a league for rookies paid so little that he had next to nothing left after buying a bus ticket home from South Carolina. Living in a dorm was out of the question because dorm contracts extended for all three quarters. The deprivations of minor league baseball life had lowered his standards such that a rooming house a few blocks from campus seemed perfectly acceptable. One distinct advantage was that he'd have his own room after months of sharing. He'd developed a knack for finding cheap meals in the diners and cafés that the players had frequented. He also knew that he would be twenty miles or so from home and that, if he felt it necessary, he could go home on weekends where his mother would see that he was well-fed. As a registered student he could use the college's athletic facilities to stay in condition. St. Cloud State had a baseball team (also the Huskies, just like

Albany), and Canaugh searched out and made plans to practice with some players before their season started. The college players gave great deference to Canaugh who in their eyes had reached the admired status of a professional baseball player. Canaugh accepted their admiration, reluctant to tell them that a minor league baseball player like him made less than they likely did in their summer jobs, routinely endured 6-hour bus rides, and had to share motel rooms with other young men with dubious personal hygiene habits.

Canaugh started college without having a major field picked out, which was allowed by the college and commonly done. Canaugh would have declared "Baseball" as his major if the college would have let him. He had vague notions of emulating Coach Anderson, his high school coach, of being a coach and a teacher when his playing days were done, though he'd pick a field less rigorous than mathematics to teach. Canaugh searched the listings at the college employment office. He was wary of taking a job in any of the college cafeterias, although he figured that he could find some free meals by working there. He didn't care for the odors of cooking food, and he didn't want to wear a rubber apron or hairnet as those jobs seemed to require. Ideally, he wanted a job that would allow him to study at the same time. On his second visit, he saw a posting for a night watchman at Shoemaker Hall, a men's dorm, and he applied. After a short interview with the Residence Hall Director, who seemed impressed with Canaugh being a professional baseball player, Canaugh was told about the job expectations and was offered the job. The job required sitting in the dorm admin office from seven in the evening to midnight three nights a week, including some weekends, and making a round of all the hallways once per hour. Shoemaker Hall had no freshmen, just upperclassmen. Canaugh instinctively knew that supervising freshmen would likely be a time-consuming headache, and that supervising upper classmen and grad students would likely involve fewer distractions.

Fall Quarter classes were ordinary and of limited appeal, but the novelty of being a college student kept Canaugh's attention. In Winter Quarter, he registered for the only Sociology class available to him which was Criminology. Almost immediately, Canaugh was enthused about the course. He'd grown up in Albany where there was very little crime, typical of Minnesota small towns, especially one where religion was an important part of community life. Canaugh was fascinated by the data and anecdotes as to who committed crimes and why. He had perfect attendance for the class, and did well on the exams, earning his first college A grade. There were similar follow-up courses that Canaugh considered for his return next fall, most of them offered as part of a new major the college was offering in a field called Criminal Justice Studies. Canaugh never discussed with his parents his thoughts about Criminology or pursuing a career in Criminal Justice Studies. He knew his mother wanted him to become a teacher and his father wanted him to study business. "I want you to do better than me" he'd say.

Canaugh's job worked out well. On weeknights most of the dorm residents paid attention to their studies and so the hallways were quiet and Canaugh could study on the job. Friday and Saturday nights were different. Lots of students went home on weekends so the occupancy dropped by half. Those who remained sought to amuse themselves. Some guys brought girls into the dorm (not allowed except on Sunday afternoons) and while Canaugh was supposed to take action against the rule-breakers, he decided that if they were quiet and discreet, he would ignore them. Guys brought alcohol into their rooms. If they got noisy and turned up the music Canaugh would knock on the door but stay in the hallway. He'd shout, "Turn it down, we've had complaints." He didn't attempt to find out what the activity in the room was, and in compensation the habitual drinkers kept it reasonably quiet. Occasionally on a weekend night someone drank too much and got sick in the communal bathrooms. Canaugh would put "Out of Order" signs on the doors and fill out a chit requesting janitor service the next day. The combination of college students and alcohol almost guaranteed that acts of extreme stupidity would occur. Some incidents would take up his attention for most of the evening. Each incident and complaint was supposed to be entered into a watch log by the Night Watchman but Canaugh almost always skipped that step unless it involved the campus police, or the development was so notorious that the campus housing management would be looking for it.

Canaugh considered it a good job. At the end of Winter Quarter Canaugh met with his supervisor and explained why he'd be gone Spring Quarter and that he'd like the job again next fall. His boss, a grad student whose studies had somehow stalled so completely that he'd taken the full-time job in the college bureaucracy doing dorm management, assured Canaugh that he'd do his best to find a job for him. "Ya know, Shoemaker Hall had the lowest number of reported incidents during your duty nights, so that indicates you were doing a good job. It makes me look good, and I appreciate it."

With two quarters of college behind him, Canaugh turned his attention back to baseball. He'd been told that he had been promoted to the Big Spring Springers in Big Spring, Texas. It was still single-A ball so it was hardly a promotion, but to his family and Albany friends it would sound good. Canaugh took stock of his situation. He'd been pleasantly surprised to find that college was easier than he expected it would be. It was similar to baseball in that it wasn't raw talent that led to success as much as it was about preparation and focus on the task at hand. *Show up for all classes, pay attention, do the reading, and you're all the way to third base*, Canaugh decided. Albany High School, he decided, had been sufficiently rigorous so that the transition to St. Cloud State wasn't difficult. Canaugh didn't have much of a social life, living in a rooming house, working a night job, spending his free hours staying in good condition. He concluded that he didn't mind being a loner; it was just something that developed for him under the circumstances of wanting primarily to be a ballplayer.

CHAPTER 4

September 1951

Canaugh was back at the St. Cloud State campus by the second week of September. He needed to register for classes, find a place to live, and find a job. By now, he appreciated the campus atmosphere, acutely aware of its contrast to minor league baseball. In professional baseball there was always an ever-present tension of competition. In the nightly games, of course, each team wanted to win, but it was more than just the games. All players were good, and they were all trying to get better. If players didn't show improvement their career was over. Players wanted to be seen as better than other players at the same position, so that they would be the first to be promoted. Yes, players bonded as teammates, but Canaugh observed that something always seemed to be held in reserve in their relationship with each other, perhaps because the players believed that they would be gone up the ladder soon, or that their teammates would be gone before long, either up or out. Also, the players came from all over the country and the tobacco-chewing characters from south of the Mason-Dixon line seemed foreign and exotic to the quiet conformists from the Midwest, and vice versa. Professional baseball had only recently begun signing black players and players from the Caribbean. Blacks and whites had different backgrounds, and while generally friendly with each other, remained wary in their personal relationships.

The student body at St. Cloud State was comprised almost entirely of young white men and women from small towns and the Twin City suburbs. There was no noticeable atmosphere of competition or stress among the students. Most students dutifully went to their classes and did their assignments but, except for a small highly ambitious few, they didn't see themselves as competitors with the other students for advancement or for the financial rewards that come from reaching the top of the pyramid. The rhythm of the social life was different. Most students paid attention to their studies during the weekdays, and used the weekends for dating, going to watch the college teams play, or drinking beer. Ballplayers had off days usually on Mondays or Thursdays, which were often used for traveling. Drinking outings occurred randomly, with very little planning involved. Students from nearby communities or the Twin Cities often went home on weekends to work or maintain the friendships they had in high school.

Canaugh did some searching to find David Kackman, the Residence Hall Director at Shoemaker Hall who'd hired him. He learned that Kackman had been promoted to Director of Student Housing and had an office in the Administration Building. Canaugh knocked on his door and was warmly greeted. "Been promoted, huh?" Canaugh asked. "How's it going on your doctorate?"

Kackman waved his hand sheepishly and gave a quiet chuckle. "Oh, that's on the back burner for a while."

Canaugh knew right away that was a white lie, and that Kackman had settled in for a career in the campus bureaucracy. "Need a job for two quarters. Would you have anything for me?"

"Two quarters, hmmm," Kackman said. "Still chasin' the baseball dream, I take it."

Canaugh was annoyed at Kackman's skepticism about Canaugh's career. "Pitchers don't get to the bigs as quickly as position players. After all, we only play about every four days. And there's a lot to learn. The majors like pitchers that are older than me." Canaugh did his best to keep any self-doubt out of his answer.

"Two quarters," said Kackman again, as if he'd been asked for a tremendous favor. "Yeah, I got something for you that I think you'll like. Hepworth Hall, the women's dorm. It's mostly an office job, because obviously you won't be walking the halls every hour like you did last year. Same pay, pretty much the same schedule if that's what you want."

"The women's dorm? Really, is there some catch I'm not seeing here?" Canaugh asked.

"Well, many people find that Arbadella, the Residence Hall Director, can be a bit hard to deal with. The girls won't give you much trouble, except at curfew time. If you don't know, there's a curfew of ten o'clock on weeknights and midnight on weekends. If the girls aren't back by curfew you have to lock them out. Some of them get pretty upset about that. Will give you a lot of grief."

"Don't they just go stay overnight with their dates? Seems like a dumb rule to me," said Canaugh.

"Probably," said Kackman, "but I don't make the rules, and I can't change them," exhibiting his comfort with his role as college bureaucrat. "You just gotta enforce the rules. Ya want the job or not? I kinda saved it for you because you've got experience."

And I don't write anything in my nightly reports that looks like a problem needing attention, thought Canaugh, but he knew better than to say it out loud.

Within a week, Canaugh had registered for classes, found a place to live (a rooming house a little less dreary than the previous year), and had lined up a good student job. Registering so late he didn't have much choice for his classes, but he sifted through the offerings and found some classes he thought might be interesting and had limited reading and term paper-writing obligations. Canaugh felt odd to still be a freshman under the college classifications; he was 21 years old and had lived in other states for two summers now while doing an adult's job. Still, by Winter Quarter he'd be a sophomore and that seemed like progress on the academic front.

Kackman had set up a meeting for Canaugh with the Residence Hall Director Arbadella just before he had to report for work. "Is Arbadella her first name, and if so what's her last name?" he'd asked Kackman.

"It's her first," he'd responded. "If your first name is Arbadella, no one needs to know your last name. Cripes, it's not like you're going to get mistaken for someone else named Arbadella, now is it."

Arbadella was in her thirties. Canaugh thought she was a bit severe and old-fashioned in manner and her style of dress. Arbadella wasted no time setting out her expectations for her night watchmen, which she delivered with prim authority with her hands folded on her completely bare desk. "Stay in the office. No roaming around to see what you can see. That goes for outside as well as inside. If there is any incident that requires you to go into the area of the rooms, you need to call the RA, the Resident Advisor where the incident is located, to come to the office and accompany you at all times until you return to the office. The front door is to be locked at the curfew times and all students who are out past curfew are to be turned away." Canaugh could suddenly see that he was dealing with someone who didn't think about all the consequences of her rules. "Finally, and this is the most important, you are not to start dating any of the residents while you are employed here. In my experience, that just leads to trouble. Not professional," she said in a clipped tone, conveying that being professional was the most important thing to her. She looked over the top of her cat's-eye glass frames at Canaugh. "Is everything understood?"

Canaugh had the same sinking feeling as when an

unhappy manager made his first visit to the mound to give him an ultimatum. Canaugh thought it best to change the subject, and perhaps learn a little more about his new boss. "Tell me a little about yourself, and your graduate program," he ventured with the friendliest tone he could muster.

Arbadella leaned back in her chair. It was obvious she didn't like personal questions, and Canaugh right away regretted having asked. "Well," she said in a clipped tone, "I'm nearly done with coursework for my master's degree in Industrial Psychology."

Canaugh immediately sympathized with all the future employees, decades ahead, who would encounter her, get analyzed, and then probably fired by the rigid Arbadella. Canaugh wanted the job, he needed the job, and so he confined his communications with Arbadella to only smiles and nods when she showed him around the building. As he walked back to his rooming house, he thought of the irony that in playing ball he faced batters who'd played in the majors and batters who were without doubt on their way to the majors, and he didn't recall the level of intimidation he'd felt around Arbadella. Canaugh decided that he could get along with Arbadella if he just played by her rules and took no chances.

Fall Quarter passed without anything out of the ordinary for Canaugh. He went to class, did the reading, completed his assignments, and worked out daily at the Field House. He reported to work three times a week at the women's dorm wearing a white dress shirt and tie, which Arbadella required. The job allowed him time to study, and he liked not having to make rounds once an hour like in the men's dorm. One of the campus cops named Finnegan visited once each night just to check on things as part of his regular patrol beat. Finnegan, though nearing retirement age, was a baseball fan who remembered Canaugh's name from the sports pages when Canaugh was the outstanding high school pitcher in the St. Cloud area. They would chat about baseball, the favorite subject for each of them. Other than Finnegan, Canaugh led a largely solitary life on campus.

Canaugh learned to dread the curfew lock-out process. On weeknights usually nothing much happened. Weekends were different. When he went to the front door to lock it, there were often many couples standing outside, sharing a last kiss. The couples parted when Canaugh stepped out and said "Twelve o'clock" holding the ring of door keys above his head to communicate what was coming next, Canaugh figuring that no further explanation was needed. It was what came next that was stressful. Women would knock on the door after it was locked, and sometimes the males who accompanied them pounded on the door with great force. Those outside the door could see Canaugh in the office with the lights on not far away, and they wrongly assumed that he would come open the door if they just pleaded. There were two typical approaches; being nice and being obnoxious, and they seemed to be tried with equal measure, often in combination. Some would want to debate the timing ("Hey, I've still got five minutes.") This frequently happened after girls were considerably under the influence of alcohol. Sometimes, girls would shout "Please" for a while, and after a while the male would get impatient and shout something like "Hey asshole." For a while Canaugh would step to the narrow window adjacent to the door, trying to be decent, and say something like "Sorry, I just can't. Dorm rules." After a while he got tired of that approach and stopped, since it just led to either more pleading or more arguments. He would try to stay out of sight. He asked Finnegan about the dorm's rule, and whether or not it caused more problems than it was worth. Finnegan just shrugged and said, "Well Vince, there's never been an instance of any girl freezing to death on campus. Most of these girls, they only have to get locked out once and then they learn. It's a problem that solves itself eventually. Besides..." Canaugh saw Finnegan's eyes twinkle, "it's Arbadella's rule." He shrugged again.

Canaugh finished Fall Quarter. For the two-week quarter break, he signed up for a job on a cleaning crew who worked on mopping and buffing dorm floors on campus. He'd asked Kackman for a decent job and he'd been rewarded with being a supervisor. It wasn't so much that he needed the money (he always needed money) but that he didn't want to spend the two-week quarter break in Albany with nothing to do. By year-end he was halfway through the college part of his year and then the baseball part would start.

One late January Saturday night he was on duty. He'd locked the door at midnight and was getting ready to turn out the lights and punch out on the time clock as it neared 12:30. There was a pounding on the door, and he could see that there was a couple standing outside. Though he would usually ignore the door-knocking and hide at this time of the night, this time was different. There was a young woman peering in the window and on her face was not the hazy unfocused look of a coed who'd had too much to drink, but instead a look of genuine distress. She had on a nice dress coat and high heels. She was petite and very pretty. A young man was with her who had the glassy eyes found in guys who'd had too much to drink. Although well-dressed for the evening, he looked the part of a fraternity guy, not too bright but with a sense of entitlement that came from having family money. It was Canaugh's instinct that turning her away would leave her vulnerable to a guy that looked like potential trouble. Canaugh looked around both inside the lobby and outside the building and didn't see anyone. He opened the door after curfew for the first time just wide enough for the young woman to slip through, which she did with a hurry. Once inside, Canaugh locked the door quickly and told the woman "I'm not supposed to do this, but I'll make an exception for you."

She was already hurrying out of the lobby, head down. Canaugh thought he saw a look of disappointment on the guy's face. She stopped at the door which separated the lobby from the girls' rooms and turned around and made eye contact with Canaugh. "Thank you," she said quietly, her greenish eyes getting wet. "Bad date," she said with barely a smile, and then she was through the door.

In a few minutes Canaugh turned out the lights and punched out on the time clock. He walked across campus in the dark to his rooming house, the snow crunching under his feet. He thought about the greenish teary eyes he'd seen and tried to imagine everything that might have happened to the girl before the couple got to the door of Hepworth Hall that night.

CHAPTER 5

January 1952

Canaugh's next duty night at Hepworth Hall was the following Tuesday. It was a memorable night. He had barely settled into his chair and was opening his gym bag that he used as a briefcase when Arbadella burst into the office without knocking. He was surprised, because Arbadella rarely paid any of the night watchmen a visit, devoting her nights to working on her thesis in her apartment located in the basement of Hepworth Hall. She had a stern look, and without any preliminary pleasantries, she let Canaugh know what was on her mind. "I've had a report that you let one of the girls in well after curfew. Is that the case?"

Canaugh knew from the look of certainty on her face that there was no point in denying. Canaugh said, "Yes, but—" which is all he was able to say before Arbadella cut him off.

"I don't want to hear it. You're on notice and this is your final warning. If it happens again, you'll be terminated. And don't think your *buddy* Kackman can save your job. I run this dorm," she said, raising her voice and emphasizing every word in the last sentence. With that, she was gone, leaving Canaugh speechless.

Canaugh immediately began to wonder how Arbadella found out about Saturday night. For that matter he wondered how she knew that Kackman had gotten him good jobs with the college. Arbadella's omniscience was indeed impressive, and Canaugh was struck with the idea of how information provided power. After a few minutes of thought, Canaugh began to piece together how Arbadella could have obtained her information. Arbadella likely had one or more of the RA's who collected and shared information with her. It was likely the RA for the girl with the green eyes had become aware that she'd been let in the door past curfew. Canaugh didn't doubt that Arbadella, who'd had the job for several years, could have had informants among the student residents, too. As to Canaugh's friendly relationship with Kackman, the latter had probably shared stories with Arbadella. They'd had the same comfortable job as Dorm Directors for a few years and seemed to both be on the same track of making only casual progress through grad school. Given Kackman's propensity to flap his lips, it was likely easy for Arbadella to connect the dots on Kackman's friendly relationship with Canaugh.

Canaugh was a bit bothered by his confrontation with Arbadella. As a baseball player or a student, he didn't like someone in authority mad at him. He liked his campus job and figured it would be hard to find another one as suitable as this one. He settled himself by closing his eyes and taking a few deep breaths, a habit he'd learned as a pitcher to get himself focused and to dispel the tension in his muscles. Almost immediately, there was a knock on the office door. He said, "Come in" warily, afraid that it was Arbadella, coming back to deliver a second tongue-lashing.

The door opened and it was the girl with the green eyes. Unlike Saturday night, her hair was perfectly arranged, and she was smiling. She carefully advanced to the desk. "I just want to thank you for letting me in Saturday night. I hope you didn't get it trouble for it."

Canaugh hesitated a bit. He didn't have much experience talking to girls as pretty and wholesome as the one in front of him. "You're welcome. No, I didn't get in trouble. I was happy to do it." Canaugh wanted to continue the conversation, but he was afraid of being observed by Arbadella having a friendly chat with one of the residents, knowing that he was now on very thin ice with his boss. "Have a seat," he said, adding "if you don't mind, can you take that chair by the wall." It was the one chair in the office not visible to anyone passing by. The girl looked puzzled, so Canaugh said, "It's the most comfortable," and felt stupid saying so because all the chairs were identical.

After a moment of awkward silence, the girl finally said, "I'm Judy. Judy Billier."

"Vince Canaugh."

There was another interval that went on just a bit long, and Judy finally said, "The girls here say that you're a football player."

"I play baseball. In the minor leagues. Now, at least. I'm hoping that's not always the case. You ever hear of the Big Spring Springers?" Judy shook her head no. "Didn't think so. Two years ago, I hadn't heard of them either." Judy's smile caused Canaugh to relax a bit, coupled with Canaugh realizing that she was making no effort to stand up and leave. Conversation got easier after that, though Canaugh kept scanning the office window to see who might be passing by. Canaugh learned that Judy was from St. James, a farming town near the Iowa border. Her parents owned a farm. She had two older brothers, both of whom had played baseball in high school for the St. James Saints. She talked easily as she told Canaugh her life story. Canaugh was struck by how pretty she was. He'd noticed the green eyes right away when he first encountered her. She had dark brown hair which she wore somewhat short, with the ends flipped up, a popular style for college girls. She had an olive complexion, and small very white teeth. She had delicate lips and a thin nose. She apparently liked to talk. She told Canaugh that she was planning to be an education major, because her parents wanted her to become a teacher, but she was also considering other majors, too.

It dawned on Canaugh as she talked that she was interested in him. A mere expression of gratitude for his letting her in the door would have only taken a minute, but they'd been talking for over ten minutes. It was time for Canaugh to find out where he stood. He wasn't used to asking girls out so he did his best to sound casual when he said, "Could we go out sometime?" Canaugh held his breath.

She acted surprised but said, "Yes" with a smile. "When?"

Canaugh knew his schedule for the week and said, "Friday?" When she nodded yes, he added, "It has to be a secret." He could see the concern on her face and before she could say anything he explained. "I'm not supposed to date anyone who lives here in the dorm. Arbadella's rule, which is why it has to be secret. I can meet you around the corner. If that's OK." Canaugh hoped that this additional term wouldn't wreck his chances with Judy, but it didn't.

"It'll be a secret," she said in a stage whisper and laughed.

After she left the office, Canaugh started planning how he could take Judy out in St. Cloud and not get caught. They couldn't be seen by anyone who might be reporting to Arbadella, or else his night watchman job was over with. He figured, not irrationally, that Arbadella had a network of people who passed on information. He expected that due to the campus grapevine, he might have trouble getting any decent job on campus if he'd been fired for violating college rules. He pictured the alternative of himself in a rubber apron washing pots and pans in a steamy kitchen. He had to be careful.

Canaugh had arranged to meet Judy under a streetlamp on a corner a block away from her dorm. He was concerned that his need for secrecy might be off-putting to Judy, so he'd stopped in a drugstore near campus and found a pair of "Groucho Glasses", plastic eyeglass frames with a plastic nose and oversized bushy eyebrows. He was wearing the glasses as Judy approached. She laughed, hard, which Canaugh found endearing.

Canaugh had done some planning. He'd picked out a movie and timed their arrival for after the previews had started so that the theater would be dark. They sat in the back row, near the wall. Their evening ended at Albert's, an old-fashioned diner a bit away from the campus. Canaugh was familiar with it because he was a fairly regular customer for their spaghetti special. He knew that it was dimly lit in the evenings (an economy measure for the frugal Albert, the owner, and not an attempt to create any particular atmosphere). It had high dark wooden booths which furnished its customers some privacy. Canaugh found that Judy was talkative and laughed easily. His mother would say that she 'had lots of personality', an expression his mother was fond of for any person who didn't adopt the grim dutiful demeanor so common in citizens of Minnesota Catholic small towns.

Mostly he just enjoyed looking at her, enjoying her stories about her family and life on a dairy farm. Canaugh began to notice that in her rush of talking, she would make up words that fit her sentences, even if they weren't words found in the dictionary. She described herself as being a bit 'droggy' in the morning. She used words that were not actually correct but still made perfect sense. A store with high prices was described as having 'exuberant' prices. He found it charming. The evening stretched on and Canaugh began checking his watch. When Judy caught him looking at his watch he explained, "For sure, tonight, I've got to get you back to Hepworth on time."

For the long walk back through campus, Judy took his arm. When they got to the streetlamp where they had met earlier, Judy turned to face him, and while Canaugh hesitated to initiate a good night kiss, Judy kissed him. "Next weekend? Saturday night?" asked Canaugh. Judy nodded yes.

Canaugh followed behind her on her way back to Hepworth to make sure she got there safely, staying in the dark until she was through the gray metal front door. Canaugh turned and walked back to his room. He'd always been taught that in baseball you walk off the field the same way, whether you won or lost. It was one of the many unwritten rules of the game, and Canaugh faithfully lived with that rule both playing baseball and otherwise. Tonight, he didn't feel that way. He felt like jogging and punching the air on his way home, so he did, through the dark streets of St. Cloud.

His next night on duty at the dorm was Sunday night. Canaugh couldn't relax. He dreaded that Arbadella would burst through the door at any time that evening and fire him, but it never happened. On their second date, Judy was ready to join in on the fun of keeping secrets. She wore pants, a borrowed pea coat, and a stocking cap that covered up all her hair. As she approached Canaugh in the dim light he thought, at first, she was just a very small guy. When she stepped under the streetlight, they both burst out laughing at her disguise. "Vince," she said in the lowest voice that she could manage, "how's it hangin', pal?" Canaugh just snorted and laughed. To complete the ruse, he finally gave her a guy's friendly punch in the shoulder.

The second date went like the first, with Judy eager to learn more about Canaugh and his life. There were lots of laughs. At Albert's Diner, she took the seat next to him this time, and as she talked, she rested her hand on either his arm, or later, on his thigh. As he walked her back to her dorm at the end of the evening, it occurred to him that he'd never felt so happy in his life. When they got to the streetlamp, Judy stopped for a farewell kiss like the previous week, but Canaugh just quietly said, "I'll walk you to the door." He walked her all the way to the door of Hepworth Hall, and they shared several long slow kisses on the steps, with Judy removing her hat to allow her hair to fall free.

Canaugh knew Danny Schact, the nightwatchman on

duty that night. Danny was waiting on the other side of the glass, theatrically checking his watch, waiting for the midnight hour to strike. Danny saw Canaugh outside with Judy and gave him an unmistakable *what the hell ya think you're doing?* stare, but Canaugh didn't care. He was in love and it felt great.

Canaugh's next shift at the dorm was Monday. He went to work expecting the axe to fall. He couldn't study due to the tension. He spent six hours waiting for Arbadella to come through the door and gleefully can him. It didn't happen. *Is there a greater feeling,* Canaugh wondered, *than knowing that you're getting away with something?*

From that point forward, Canaugh and Judy didn't date so much as become constant companions. They had study dates at the college library, making some accommodations to their forbidden relationship. They would sit two tables apart, facing each other, giving each other discreet (they hoped) smiles when they looked up from their books. When it was time to leave, they would leave the reading room at separate times and meet outside on the front steps. It was difficult to avoid being seen together in public, but with a little planning and effort it worked out. Canaugh, a couple of times, got a ride home on weekends with fellow students for the thirty miles or so to Albany. He would borrow the family car from his puzzled parents, which he drove back to campus and used to take Judy out to dinner or a movie in nearby towns of Sartell and Sauk Rapids. Though women were prohibited in his rooming house, by February Canaugh had learned the rhythms of his fellow residents and could sneak Judy into his room without anyone noticing. He would turn up his GE clock radio so that no one could overhear them. Their relationship was intense, made so by their attraction to each other and most of all, by the knowledge that Canaugh would leave college after Winter Quarter and be gone most of the spring and all of the summer. They likely wouldn't see each other again until the end of August.

St. Cloud State College had its own rhythms. Final exams

were set for the week after classes end, in mid-March. Social life greatly diminished the last week or two of classes because most students stopped procrastinating, found their reading lists, and got serious about studying. Canaugh was still scheduled three nights a week for his job, but it wasn't a burden because he could study on the job. Because most residents were studying, there was very little that needed his attention. His presence in the dorm allowed Judy to pop into his office to bring him some Hershey's candy kisses with a wink, or step in and furtively blow him a kiss. Canaugh and Judy were busy the last two weeks studying for and taking their exams, so they saw very little of each other.

On his last night on duty, Canaugh was weary after two weeks of studying, working, and taking exams. The dorm was mostly empty, because most students took off for Spring Break as soon as their last exam was behind them. He was surprised when Arbadella appeared in his office, sat down, and started a conversation about turning in his badge and obtaining an address where his last paycheck could be mailed. Canaugh thought that their chat would be limited to final arrangements when she said, "I've become aware of your relationship with Judy Billier. Some time ago, if you must know. It was against my rule, but I decided to do nothing because you two were working so hard to keep it secret. You didn't flaunt it, so it didn't embarrass me or cause me any problems." She paused, obviously reluctant to say something. "Besides," she said, "I like you both. I think you make a good couple."

Canaugh's mouth was open, but he was unable to say anything in light of her uncharacteristically human remarks. Finally, it occurred to him that the appropriate thing to say was thank you, which he did.

"Good luck with your baseball, and maybe we will see you again," she said as she rose without smiling and offered Canaugh a very firm handshake.

There were only a few days left after spring break when Canaugh was supposed to report to the Montgomery Rebels in Montgomery, Alabama, for the start of spring training. Judy fibbed to her parents that she needed to stay on in St. Cloud a few days. The dorms were closed but she had a friend who let her stay in her apartment. Canaugh wasn't inclined to try to stay with her, either at the rooming house or the apartment. They spent what time they could together. She watched as Canaugh packed a suitcase with his clothes and his all-purpose gym bag with his personal baseball gear including spikes, glove, and jock strap. She walked with him to downtown St. Cloud to the bus station and they bade a tender farewell, with promises to call and write as much as possible. As the bus headed down to Minneapolis, Canaugh figured that he'd found the person he wanted to spend his life with, a thought he'd never even considered before.

CHAPTER 6

August 1952

Betrothed read the caption under Judy's photo in the St. James Plaindealer. "Betrothed? Canaugh asked Judy. "Why do newspapers still say that? Do people really use that word anymore?" He'd just finished reading the clipping that Judy had mailed to him. He was calling from the Sandman Motel in Montgomery. His team had just returned from a road trip and his mail was waiting for him.

"What term does the hometown paper use in Albany," she asked.

"Hitched. It's a very rural place, y'know." Judy's laugh was like music to Canaugh. Judy looked very pretty in her engagement photo, taken at the March Studio on Main Street in St. James. The photographer's dab of Vaseline on her cheeks made them shiny in the photo. The engagement notice stated that Judy's fiancée was 'a professional athlete in the Washington Senators' organization.' Canaugh read the words to Judy slowly with obvious skepticism.

"That was my mother's idea. She's the one who put it in the paper. She wanted you to sound important."

"Well, I guess it's a bit more dignified than saying that he's some jock who's been in the minors for 4 years and he's still at double-A ball getting paid five hundred bucks a month and hoping for a break."

Canaugh was still slowly getting used to the fact that though he was only 22 years old, he was getting married in a few months. Judy had graduated from college in June, her commencement being one more big event in her life that Canaugh had missed because he was playing ball somewhere a thousand miles away. Finding a teaching job wasn't easy, but Judy was glad to have found one in St. Paul. Teaching didn't pay that well, but as she and Canaugh had decided, *It's a start.* A lot had happened since Judy and Canaugh had met each other a little over two years ago. Canaugh continued to play minor league baseball for half the year in the Senators' organization. He'd made the move up from single-A to double-A baseball. Canaugh would explain the difference to anyone who asked by saying that 'the living conditions and pay aren't much better, but at least the hitters you face are better.'

Canaugh continued work on his degree in Criminology at St. Cloud State two quarters a year but planned to transfer to the University of Minnesota once they moved to St. Paul. Judy, who'd started a year behind him had caught up and passed him. Canaugh took one winter quarter off to work loading trucks to earn money to buy a car and an engagement ring. "Both small," he told Judy. "But at least the engagement ring is new." The wedding had been planned for Labor Day weekend, just before Judy's job started. Judy and Canaugh found a small apartment on the second floor of a house in St. Paul.

Judy's youthful innocence charmed Canaugh. He once introduced her to his friend Dick, another Minnesota minor league ballplayer who worked out with him in the offseason. "Dick, this is my girlfriend Judy," Canaugh had said.

Dick sized up her wholesome farmer's daughter appearance and said, "You look like a Judy."

Canaugh continued the introduction by saying, "Judy, this is my buddy, Dick."

Judy looked him over and said, "You look like a Dick."

Dick and Canaugh both tried to hold in their laughter at Judy's response, but it spilled out in guffaws. Judy was mystified at the response of the two young men. Canaugh could only deal with it by leading Judy away from Dick, who was unable to stop laughing.

Canaugh's baseball career teetered between his feeling that he wasn't good enough to stick with it and a feeling that he was on track for bigger and better things. Baseball's bromides, repeated by coaches and his teammates, kept his spirits afloat. 'They always need lefties' gave him hope. So did 'It takes a while for pitchers to develop before they're ready for the big leagues.' At the start of games, when he was announced as the starting pitcher, he felt a rush of pride, even though in many minor-league parks the PA system speakers were fuzzy and sometimes screeched. When he played on some other team's home field, he sometimes got announced as 'Vince Can-Ogg' because in the rural south Irish names were less common. A good night on the mound gave him cheer. A night when the batters were hitting his pitches and the ump's strike zone couldn't be deciphered would send him into a deep funk.

To advance up the ladder in baseball, a pitcher needed more than just to have a good fastball or curve, like Canaugh had in high school. The hitters wanted to reach the big leagues as much as the pitchers did, and they were experienced and capable. Canaugh worked with his coaches to develop a third pitch to add to his repertoire. It took time but eventually he developed his ability to throw a slider with confidence that it would go exactly where he wanted it to go. Once he had command of three pitches, the coaches wanted him to develop a fourth pitch.

In professional baseball, merely throwing the ball with speed exactly where you wanted it to go, never an easy skill to learn, was only part of the skills a pitcher needed to develop.

Pitching, to a great extent, was about fooling hitters and keeping them off balance. Hitters could hit all but the fastest pitches, particularly if they came straight as a straw from the pitcher's hand. Therefore, the pitcher had to learn to put movement on fastballs and to change speeds on all pitches. The pitcher also had to develop a good ability to guess what the hitter was expecting and, if possible, do the unexpected. Determining what the hitter was expecting was a difficult calculus dependent on many things, including how many outs there were, what the count was in terms of balls and strikes, what the batter had seen from this pitcher before, and whether there was a runner on first that affected the pitcher's priorities. For example, most batters believe that when a runner on first was likely to steal second, a pitcher was less likely to throw an off-speed pitch because it would give the runner more time to reach second. Pitchers had to learn how to experiment with a batter if they were ahead in the count and see if they would swing at a high pitch or chase a pitch in the dirt. Even minor league teams had scouting reports and so pitchers and catchers had to learn and remember the strengths and weaknesses of the batters they would face.

A pitcher also had to learn that he had a role to play as a defensive player. Pitchers were relieved of some duties they had in high school, such as being responsible to catch pop-ups anywhere in the infield. Pitchers did have to practice fielding bunts that came back to the mound. Learning how to do so perfectly became more critical in professional baseball when most every player could run fast. Learning to be in the right place all the time, such as backing up the catcher or covering first when the first baseman was fielding the ball was critical. The degree of learning necessary, in the expectation of the coaches trying to develop the abilities of minor leaguers, was to have the players ready to do things by reflex, without any need for thinking. Baseball, for most players, was learned by repetition and study. Pitchers had time to study the game in their days in the dugout, but because starting pitchers played only every fourth or fifth game, development took time. Bullpen pitchers played more often, but pitchers chosen for the bullpen were considered to be inferior to starting pitchers. It was rare for a pitcher to be given bullpen duty, and then be chosen to be a starting pitcher again, and so Canaugh dreaded being chosen for that assignment.

Judy's parents had been cheerful and enthusiastic when Judy and Canaugh had traveled to Judy's home the previous March to announce their engagement. Parents in that era hoped that their daughters would find a husband before the age of 22. It helped a great deal that Canaugh was also a small-town Catholic. To Judy's father, a farmer, Canaugh's baseball dream seemed frivolous. It was after Vince left to start the season that her parents began to ask questions about the wisdom of Judy's choice. "Is he going to be gone half the year or will he give up on baseball?" "How will he support you after he's done playing baseball?" As the days went by, Judy's answers apparently didn't allay their concerns, so the questions were stepped up a notch. "Do you really know what you're getting into?" "Do you think you're going to be happy?"

Judy had relayed these questions to Canaugh in a long-distance phone call to where his team had gathered. However, she assured him that the questions didn't change her mind about getting married. It was only after the call was over and Canaugh lay on his bed in the dark that he realized he didn't have answers to any of the questions. There were two things he wanted most in life. To succeed at baseball and to be married to Judy, and the questions of Judy's parents made him acknowledge that they could soon be in conflict. He didn't want to give up on either one. He dreaded the thought that someday he might have to choose.

It was an unusually hot Saturday in St. James on the couple's wedding day. September in southern Minnesota can be hot, some years more summer than fall. Judy's parents may have had misgivings about the union that was about to take place, but they carried on in a happy and upbeat fashion. Canaugh's side of the church was not that full. The bride's side eventually overflowed onto the groom's side, a tolerable breach of small-town etiquette under the circumstances. Small town Catholic weddings have widely different components. The ceremony is formal, embedded within a Mass that in the hands of most priests, is stiff and joyless. A reception typically follows, and its form will differ depending upon the social aspirations of the bride's parents. Some families choose a wedding dance, usually held in a dance hall with a polka band and a cash bar which does an astonishing amount of business. The Billiers chose a more sedate reception in the church basement with a buffet sandwich lunch. Afterwards only a portion of the crowd, close friends and family, were personally invited back to the Billier farm where women gathered in the house for coffee and brownies and the men caucused in the machine shed well into the evening with a keg of Grain Belt.

Canaugh and Judy escaped the reception early, headed for the Holiday Inn in Mankato, where they could enjoy having actual sex in lieu of the awkward approximations they had practiced for the past couple years. Before Canaugh fell asleep, he considered it the happiest day of his life.

CHAPTER 7

November 1952

Canaugh took stock of his situation. He was now 22 years old and newly married. Judy had obtained a job in the St. Paul school system, teaching fourth graders who lived in the Battle Creek neighborhood. He decided that teaching was like baseball, and perhaps like every other job in America. You were expected to start at the bottom and use your abilities to climb the ladder. Teachers with seniority had opted to transfer to schools in better neighborhoods, where parents valued education and set expectations for the children to do well in school. New teachers started in the working class and immigrant neighborhoods where only some of the parents set out expectations for their children. A good many of the parents were too distressed with the conditions in their lives that they couldn't pay attention to their kids' education. Keeping the kids attentive in the classroom and motivating them to learn was a bigger part of the job than Judy had expected. As she and Canaugh agreed out loud, on a regular basis, her teaching job was a necessary paycheck that allowed them to get started in life. "It won't be like this forever" Judy would say after a particularly hard day or even a hard week. Canaugh felt bad that Judy's job was hard, and that she had unhappy moments. He was still committed to playing baseball. He reasoned that if he quit baseball and found a regular job that Judy would still be teaching at the same school and having the same problems. Canaugh continued going to college in the off-season at the University of Minnesota. He got a part-time job sufficient to pay his tuition and college expenses. He worked out in the University Fieldhouse, a large barn-like building with a dirt floor. The Gopher baseball coach was happy to let him, in exchange for his sharing what he'd learned with the University pitchers who also worked out with him. As newlyweds, just barely covering expenses was sufficient, because they were happy to be together. They both enjoyed having passionate sex in the tiny bedroom of their small apartment on Cleveland Avenue.

Canaugh would take the 16A bus along University Avenue each day to the campus, carrying with him all day in a gym bag his books, his workout clothes, and the lunch Judy had packed for him. He wanted Judy to drive to school rather than take the bus, because in Minnesota winters, it's dark when you go to work and it's dark when you come home, and he wanted her to be safe. Judy clipped grocery store coupons from the paper and the neighborhood shopper. For entertainment they would walk eight blocks to the Grandview Theater to see movies. Sometimes for entertainment, they would buy and share a bottle of wine and watch TV. To them, it seemed enough. Just scraping by didn't diminish the joy in their lives.

As fall turned into winter, neither of them wanted to think about the coming baseball season and how Canaugh would be absent for six months. As for finding a way for Judy to accompany him, all he could say was "We'll see. I'm not sure where I'll be playing or what my situation would be."

Quitting baseball wasn't an option as far as Canaugh was concerned. He'd been playing professional baseball for four years. He'd been playing baseball since he was six, when his parents had wrapped up a flat pocketless glove from Montgomery Wards as his sixth birthday present. He had been one out of only four guys in the whole state of Minnesota who had been signed to minor league contracts the year he'd graduated from high school. He reviewed the ladder that he was climbing. Unlike most jobs, in baseball letters are used to clearly mark one's steps up the ladder. Low-A and High-A were the first two steps he'd made. Ahead of him were Double A, Triple-A, and the majors. Each level required more ability, more experience, and more baseball knowledge. There were players in baseball, past and current, who'd jumped up the ladder to the big leagues, sometimes missing rungs along the way. Those players with the ability to do that tended to end up in the Hall of Fame. Canaugh knew he wasn't at that level of ability and never would be. Rather, most players in baseball were grinders, players who climbed the ladder slowly with stops at each level, sometimes with occasional setbacks and slumps. The formula for advancement for those players without extraordinary ability was well known and was made clear to the players by coaches and those employed in the organization. Work hard, listen to your coaches, learn all you can, get along with others, figure out how get better every day, and manage your personal life so that it doesn't distract from baseball. Most of those lessons, Canaugh decided, applied to all occupations, though it seemed to him that not many people in regular jobs heeded these principles. Baseball was different than most jobs. There was little room for ordinary performance. You were either moving up or you were moving out because there were numerous talented players behind you on the ladder. You wanted to keep being labelled as a "prospect." As to what happened to the guys who never made it to the majors, they joined the forgotten army of professional baseball players. No one kept track of them.

Baseball was different than other jobs in the way that people got paid. The players at the top of the pyramid in the major leagues got paid well, but other players underneath them didn't get paid well at all. The salaries that got paid to the stars on the teams made the papers. There was no collective bargaining unit and there was no major league minimum. A minimum salary wouldn't come for fifteen more years, and even when that happened it was only $6,000. Many players in the major leagues found it necessary to get a job in the off-season. Players in the minors got paid very little, which fact was not widely known by baseball fans. It was a function of supply and demand. There were plenty of players who wanted to make the teams and very few positions available. Minor league teams didn't make much money. Minor league ballparks weren't large and ticket prices weren't high because the sporting public had limited interest in attending the games. In the American small towns of the lower-level minor leagues, baseball competed with the movies for available entertainment and therefore ticket prices for each tended to be about the same. In the minor league towns, the fans worked in factories and on farms and therefore they had to be careful with their money. The concession stands, other than the beer vendors, did only a middling business. The players learned to be careful with their money also. Some didn't even have cars. Players all shared motel rooms on the road and shared apartments, sometimes with 3 or 4 others, in the team's hometown. There weren't that many married players, but it was not unusual for married couples to share an apartment to save on expenses. Baseball for most, Canaugh decided, was a labor of love, but then so were many other ways that people chose for their life's work.

The season ahead felt different to Canaugh. He was married now and felt some responsibility to take care of his wife. His parents weren't that knowledgeable about baseball and seemed mostly concerned with village life in Albany and their declining health. Whatever he did in baseball was fine with them, even if that meant giving it up. His athletic accomplishments had already given them a lot of status in Albany. His new in-laws were more difficult to read. They seemed to take some pride in telling others that their daughter had married a professional baseball player. However, they also seemed to convey to him that playing ball wasn't really a respectable way to make a living, except possibly at the major league level. It was implied in ways large and small that their pretty and smart daughter deserved to be well taken care of financially. While they gave nice gifts to Judy at Christmas and her birthday, they didn't provide any other financial support to the couple.

Canaugh knew that he was pursuing a dream. Prior to getting married, he felt comfortable with the time and effort he was putting into baseball. He realized that he'd grown up with almost nothing, the son of a handyman and a store clerk in a Minnesota small town. Therefore, living on the edge financially by playing ball had always seemed to him to be a tolerable risk. *If you have nothing, you risk nothing,* he had explained it to himself. Getting married changed that risk because he was now responsible for one other person. He would try to banish the thought from his mind when it appeared. Self-doubt is the enemy of the competing athlete, he knew. He decided that there were two absolutes to guide him. He wanted to be married to Judy. He wanted to make it to the major leagues.

CHAPTER 8

September 1954

After two years of marriage, Judy had decided that she wanted a baby. They had splurged for an anniversary dinner at the Lexington, St. Paul's oldest and nicest restaurant, though they ordered the chicken pot pie instead of steaks. Judy had chosen the evening to tell Canaugh of her desire to have a child. "I'm almost 25. It's time. All my friends are having kids. My parents are dropping hints."

"Ha," replied Canaugh. "Your parents don't drop hints. A 'hint' isn't a concept they're remotely familiar with."

"That's not quite right. Anyway, are you saying you don't agree?"

"I'm all for it. When we get home, I'll make my position clear. Quite clear. Maybe we should ask for the check now."

That fall and winter the couple made an effort to make love as often as possible. Canaugh enjoyed Judy's revived interest in sex. Judy talked openly of wanting a boy who could become a ballplayer 'like his Daddy.' After a couple of months, Canaugh figured out that Judy was keeping track by making tiny red dots on a calendar she kept on the refrigerator. When they were both home a few nights later, he studied the calendar at great length, rubbing his chin while she fixed dinner. "What ya doing," she finally asked.

He responded, "Just trying to compute my batting average." She laughed, embarrassed that her record-keeping system had been discovered.

"Well, a good-looking ballplayer I know once told me 'The game is all about stats.'"

Later that winter, when the calendar turned over from February to March, Judy was disappointed. She wasn't pregnant, and she was facing the part of the year when Canaugh went off to play ball for the summer. She had come to quietly dislike being alone for the summer but didn't want to complain. She knew that her husband might give up baseball if she made an issue of it. She was aware that he would likely do that for her. Out of her love for him, she wanted him to take his talents in baseball as far as he could. Out of practical calculation, she didn't want the blame of asking him to quit to become a cloud on their marriage that might never go away. With a lot of discussion, they figured out how they might get together during the baseball season for additional baby-making opportunities. It was just an idea at first. One could hardly call it a "plan" because it had a lot of contingencies. "I'm not sure where I'll be playing" Canaugh would say. "I might get called up to triple A. I could get traded to another team. There's nothing that's ever guaranteed for any ballplayer."

The couple looked at the summer schedule for the Raleigh Capitals, where Canaugh thought he would most likely be playing. A visit by Judy would have to be on his team's homestand, and not when the team was traveling to its away games. Getting Judy to Raleigh would involve a bit of planning. The nearest big city with an airport that either Northwest or North Central had flights to was Charlotte. The couple spent some time calculating the cost because money was always tight. They would need money for airfare and for their own room and meals. "I could take a Greyhound," Judy offered once as a cost-saving measure.

"No, you won't." responded Canaugh firmly, having taken too many long bus rides and seen too many grimy and sometimes scary bus stations, frequently in some marginal neighborhood.

The plan was to make one visit for sure. Judy told Canaugh that her parents might possibly pay for a second visit. Canaugh was torn about that prospect. He would be excited to see her and happy to spend time with her. However, in order to pry money loose from his in-laws it could likely involve Judy making the disclosure to them that the purpose of the trip was mainly to get her pregnant. That type of discussion was mortifying to Canaugh. Perhaps Minnesota farmers had a more matter-of-fact approach to breeding than he did. He was aware that farmers transported cows and horses around from farm to farm for that very purpose.

Canaugh didn't get traded or promoted by July that summer so that Judy and Canaugh could proceed with the plan to have her join Canaugh for a visit. Judy made her visit to Raleigh in July. It worked out that she could stay for a week while the Capitals entertained both Chattanooga and Jacksonville for back-to-back three-game series. Canaugh didn't want Judy around the motel where most of the guys on the team stayed so he made reservations at the MarKay Hotel in downtown Raleigh. The MarKay was a three-story brick hotel, a relic from the twenties. When it was built, it was the finest place to stay in the Raleigh-Durham area.

Canaugh had made a personal visit to the MarKay to make a reservation while wearing his team jersey, hoping that the desk clerk might grant a bargain rate to a member of the local ball team. The price quoted for a one-week stay was tolerable to Canaugh, who didn't know if he was getting a deal or not. Canaugh, in his first visit to the hotel, was a bit disappointed in the condition of the hotel, because it appeared that the original carpeting and furnishings were still in use, despite being a bit worn and dated. Like the Curtis Hotel in Minneapolis, where he had once stayed for the state baseball tournament, big traditional downtown hotels from the twenties were reaching the end of their life cycle. Travelers now wanted to stay in newer places like Howard Johnson's or Holiday Inns, close to the interstate highways and benefitting from a perception of being modern and therefore better.

When Judy arrived, the couple dropped their luggage off and then had a hamburger and a beer in the hotel coffee shop. They had much to discuss. Judy, as usual, took over the conversation to cover things that she and Canaugh hadn't discussed by phone and her impressions of her first airplane trip.

Their room was large, though a bit dark with old-fashioned white tile and even more old-fashioned plumbing fixtures. Canaugh kept a close eye on Judy's reaction to the hotel. "I think they like to decorate with antiques," he fibbed to her, though she didn't challenge his conclusion. He was relieved that she was passing no judgment on their lodgings for the week. He long ago found that Judy was different from many other girls in that way. If she had higher expectations, she didn't show any disappointment. Despite the hotel's claim to be air-conditioned, the air-conditioning system, like the lobby furniture, was also from another era. While it delivered air that was cooler than the air outside, it wasn't the same that was found in new buildings.

Returning to their room, Judy and Canaugh didn't even bother to turn on the lights. Judy put her arms around Canaugh's neck and said, like infielders say in high school games, "Come on big fella, rock and fire." Canaugh laughed out loud as he unbuttoned her blouse. Their lovemaking was extended and passionate, both of them joyful to be together after an absence of several months. When they finished, they were both glistening with perspiration. Judy rolled over on her back and said to the ceiling. "We want a pitcher, not a belly-itcher."

"Where did that come from?" asked Canaugh.

"Oh, when my brothers played Legion ball in the summer, the other teams would sometimes come up from Iowa. My friends and I would sit on the bleachers and yell that at the Iowa pitchers. Everyone thought it was funny."

"Why now." asked Canaugh.

Judy was quiet for a minute and then said, "You know that I want to have a boy just like you. So, I guess it was just a wish." They were both quiet for another minute or two and then she said, "Just a prayer."

CHAPTER 9

July 1954

Canaugh spent the summer of 1954 mostly with the Raleigh Capitals, the double A affiliate of the Washington Senators. He started the season well, with a 4-1 record and an ERA just over 3.0. He was hoping for a promotion, and it finally happened in late June, when he was reassigned to the Denver Bears, the triple A affiliate of the Washington Senators. The Bears played in the American Association, whose teams included the Minneapolis Millers and the St. Paul Saints. Canaugh was delighted to know that if he could stick with the team, road trips would include a week in Minnesota, playing both Twin City teams. He'd be able to stay with Judy in their apartment on Cleveland Avenue. Depending on the timing, he'd likely have to pitch twice in his one week in Minnesota, but the rest would be like a honeymoon, he figured. Given Judy's desire to get pregnant, Canaugh told Judy in their excited phone call that they'd be able to work on that goal nightly. "Morningly, too" he told Judy. That wasn't a word, he knew, but she had her own vocabulary of novel words, so he felt free to make one up also. His joke made her laugh.

Canaugh, who liked to read baseball history, was aware that a lot of great players had spent time playing in the American Association, including Ted Williams, Mickey Mantle, and Willie

Mays. It was the gateway to the majors for a lot of players. Playing in the American Association meant traveling by plane for the first time. He was filled with enthusiasm that he was on the way to the majors, and his six years in minor league ball had all been worth it. The chest-swelling optimism he'd felt when he was eighteen and signed his first contract returned for several days. He remembered how he felt as he headed for Hampton, Virginia and the Peninsula Pilots, his first team.

On his way to Denver, Canaugh recalled his journey through the minor league teams. He'd worn a lot of uniforms and sat in a lot of dugouts. He'd started with the Peninsula Pilots in Virginia. His rookie season was in retrospect mostly spent unlearning what he'd learned in high school, and then learning new things that were expected in professional baseball. Everything seemed different to Canaugh. Much was made of the mechanics of pitching. It started with how to hold his glove and the ball in the approved way while he got the signs from the catcher. The coaches changed his delivery motion a bit. There were also dimensions to pitching that he'd never consciously thought of before, such as arm slot choice, ball concealment, stride, and follow-through. He learned about proper warm-up and care of his arm. Professional baseball, he learned, was all about two things: constant vigilance to find tiny advantages, and then constant repetition to ensure perfect duplication of every motion.

The scrutiny the ballplayers received was a sizable change from high school. In high school, coaches had only basic expertise in the sport at best. Coaching baseball, for small-town coaches in Minnesota, was often just an afterthought to also coaching the main high school sports of football and basketball. Coaches often had to fit their baseball duties in along with their other roles of teacher, husband, and father. Minor league coaches had all been players, though very few had ever reached the major leagues. Most coaches Canaugh encountered had the baseball knowledge and the insight to know what made the difference between a player that was ready to climb the ladder to a higher level and one that needed corrective work.

Professional coaches had learned to look for the little things that ballplayers do. For pitchers, they looked for things that would tip a batter off as to what the pitcher was going to throw next. Canaugh found it nerve-wracking to have one or two coaches standing nearby watching him for half an hour as he threw in the bullpen.

Canaugh's first season was spent with the Pilots in the rookie league. It was standard that all players spent a whole season with their assigned team their rookie year. No one moved up. There was a lot for the organizations to learn about the players they had signed. There was a lot for the players to learn, not only about baseball, but also about the job of playing baseball. In high school and Legion baseball, players played two games a week and from time to time, if the team was in a tournament, they might have played three days in a row. In the minors, the players had to adjust to playing six days a week, with usually a practice session on the day off. Baseball as a job was something one had to learn. Minor league baseball had its own deprivations. Bus travel, loneliness, boredom, and trying to eat well with only small-town diners as an option.

After Canaugh's first season with the Pilots, he was assigned to the Greenville Spinners in Greenville, South Carolina. It was still a single-A ball team in a southern town, and so he was unsure if it was a promotion or not. The word from players and coaches was that playing for the Spinners wasn't a promotion, but rather was considered "seasoning." When Canaugh would hear the term, he would think of his mother making a pot roast dinner and discussing the need for more seasoning. Canaugh spent the whole season with the Spinners, and next year was assigned to the Big Spring Springers in Big Spring, Texas.

He spent most of that season with the Springers, learning

from experience. When his Minnesota friends and relatives would ask him what he learned from the season, he'd reply, "It gets goddamn hot in Texas." The next year he got promoted to the Montgomery Rebels in Montgomery, Alabama. He was happy for a couple of reasons. He no longer had to live in the arid and colorless world of west Texas. The Rebels were a double-A team, a sign that his organization thought that he was developing. Frequently he was told that it takes longer for pitchers to develop than the position players, and that he should be patient. He was still a starting pitcher, which was reassuring to him. Starting pitchers were considered better than relievers. He did all right in Montgomery and was glad when they told him that he'd return to Montgomery next spring. He liked Montgomery, the capital city of Alabama. A small city, it reminded him in many ways of St. Paul, the capital city of Minnesota. In addition to having a capitol building, it had leafy streets, lots of brick buildings, and gracious homes. The people he met were friendly and hospitable. He spent the whole summer in Montgomery. He had a respectable won-loss record and earned the respect of his coaches.

The next season he was assigned to the Raleigh Capitals in Raleigh, North Carolina. The move from one double-A team (Montgomery) to another (Raleigh) didn't seem to Canaugh like much of a promotion, but his manager at Raleigh took him aside early on and explained that Raleigh was the closest double-A team to the major league club in Washington. For that reason, he could expect to get more exposure to the top scouts and team executives of the Senators who liked to visit Raleigh to play golf during the day and watch games at night and call it a hard day's work. Canaugh was skeptical at first, but then decided that perhaps that was the reason he'd been selected to go to Denver.

Canaugh had a surprise when he got to Denver and had his first meeting with the pitching staff and Clayton Kleiber, the Bears' pitching coach. He was told that he'd see a difference pitching in Denver. Unlike pitching in the humid, swampy night air in the cities of the South, pitching in the mile-high altitude of Denver favored the batters over the pitcher. The elevation and dry air permitted a batted ball to carry a lot further. "Pop flies here often land on the far side of the fence" was how it was explained to him. It would have helped the pitchers if the home run fence had been moved back to account for the difference in elevation between Denver and the Midwest cities in the American Association, but the owners of the Denver club learned that home runs and high scoring games sell a lot of tickets and therefore kept their ballpark dimensions at standard size.

Canaugh, for the first time in his career, had little success on the mound. He didn't win any games and frequently pitched only three or four innings before the manager came to the mound to replace him. Canaugh, like all starting pitchers, felt miserable handing over the ball to the manager, in baseball's most painful ritual. It wasn't just the long hits in the thin air that caused his problems, it seemed to him. "I just can't get anyone out," he said to Judy in a long phone call after he'd been in Denver a month. "The hitters are just that much better than in double-A ball."

"Just stick with it" was Judy's response. "The guy I married will find a way to get better." Canaugh appreciated Judy's pep talk and her faith in him. The cold truth was that the hitters were that much better. In triple-A ball, there were guys who'd made it to the majors and for various reasons weren't quite good enough. There were major league players who were coming back from injuries and needed to rehab. There were former major league players who weren't headed back to the big leagues, but either couldn't give up the game or else were deluded by their own hopes that they could make it back to the majors. There were plenty of young minor league players who were on their way to the big leagues and would get there with a little more seasoning. As the end of the season neared, the manager came to Canaugh and asked him if he'd be okay with going to the bullpen as a reliever. Canaugh realized that the skipper didn't have to ask him, he could have just told him of the change. Canaugh figured that the manager was being diplomatic because he liked him, or he respected Canaugh's many years in the minors. Though he felt overwhelming emotions of shame and embarrassment, he said, "Sure, skip, if it will keep me here." The manager just nodded, feeling as awkward about the conversation as Canaugh did.

Though Canaugh finished the season in Denver, he was highly apprehensive about next season. He was not surprised when he was notified that he was being assigned to the Wisconsin Rapids Senators in northern Wisconsin, a double-A team. He told Judy his interpretation of the move. "The organization has lost faith in me. They're being kind, and by keeping me close to Minnesota instead of sending me off to some ass-backwards town down South." After feeling morose for a few days, he told Judy for the first time ever that it was time to think realistically about giving up on baseball and doing something else. He was surprised by her response.

"Oh, hell no," she said, using profanity for the first time ever with Canaugh. "You can't give up. You have to give it at least one more year. Don'tcha see? I don't want a husband with any regrets. One who's gonna mope around for the next fifty years saying 'woulda, coulda, shoulda'. Go play for the Wisconsin Rabbits, whoever the heck they are. It can't be more than a hundred miles away. I'll get a job there if I need to, or if I can't, I'll come visit on weekends. We can at least spend one summer together. I'll even go back to Denver with you, which I bet's gonna happen."

Canaugh later studied the road atlas that their State Farm agent had given the couple at Christmas. Wisconsin Rapids was 185 miles from St. Paul. It was his eighth year in professional baseball, but Canaugh remembered it from then on as the year that everything changed. On an apartment-hunting trip to Wisconsin Rapids that spring, he and Judy found a furnished room to rent in a large old home owned by an unsmiling widow named Mrs. Gallagher.

"I don't usually rent to ballplayers, but seeing how you're married and you're Catholics, I'll make an exception," she'd said grimly. Their room was on the second floor of the house, right over Mrs. Gallagher's bedroom on the first floor. Judy was still determined to start a family, and they made love with enthusiasm almost nightly when the team was in town. The springs on the ancient bed squeaked so much that Canaugh was glad Mrs. Gallagher was nearly deaf and doubly glad that she fell asleep early. Judy found a job as a cashier and clerk in the Ben Franklin store on Main Street. Her minimum wage job and Canaugh's pay from the Senators allowed them to break even financially, despite having to also pay the rent for the apartment in St. Paul.

Canaugh regained a spot in the rotation as a starting pitcher. He was relieved to find that he could still get double-A batters out, and his record and stats were respectable. However, he realized that he was 26 years old and that he was getting to be one of the older minor league pitchers. He was the second oldest player on the team. Perhaps it was his imagination at work, but he thought that the coaches and players looked at him a bit differently now that he'd been up to triple-A and had been sent back down. He was no longer considered a prospect. Canaugh considered that there was little more that he could learn about the game. He'd added all the muscle he needed to be fully grown by his hours in the weight room. He doubted that there was any way he could improve as a pitcher.

Canaugh noticed something else about himself. On the nights when he wasn't pitching or charting pitches, he would from time to time get bored with the game in process. That had never happened before. He didn't spend as much time interacting with his teammates as in years past. He celebrated the team's wins with minimal joy and tended to disregard both his own and the team's losses. He recognized these small signs of his detachment from playing ball.

He also found that he enjoyed his time with Judy more than ever. Since their marriage, they'd never spent a summer together. Little things they'd never done before, like going out for ice cream cones, or going to the beach for a swim, were delightful novelties, something they both enjoyed.

As the season was coming to an end, Canaugh came to the realization that he could now leave the game without any regrets about giving it up. He had regrets that he'd never made it to the majors and never even in fact succeeded at triple-A. Professional baseball, he'd decided, was all about aspiration. Every player he'd met in his last eight years was aspiring to improve, to do well, to move up to a higher club, to make it to the majors. It was the promise of future success that kept everyone in the game, despite the low pay and all the deprivations that come with being broke and spending lonely summers in small towns across the country. However, Canaugh concluded, once you stop aspiring, you're not really participating any more. You're an anomaly, an outlier, you don't fit in. There's no real place for you in the game. It was time to give it up.

What was he giving up? Canaugh took inventory as to what he'd remember about being on a minor league baseball team. The smell of sweat, chewing tobacco, and farts. Hellos and farewells, friendships and fights, arguments, jokes, elation, and disappointment. Bus rides, card games, loneliness, boredom, and the tense anticipation before the start of each game. There was the smell of leather in the gloves and balls, different whether wet or dry. The sound wooden bats made, very different whether hitting the ball or the concrete floor of the dugout.

There were the holy and constant numbers of the game; nine innings, 90 feet between bases, 60 feet six inches from the pitching rubber to home plate, five ounces for a baseball, twenty-seven outs for a complete game. Above all, there was the unspoken respect for the game by those who still played it.

CHAPTER 10

January 1957

Once his days playing professional baseball were behind him, Canaugh applied for and was selected to join the Minneapolis Police Department. Becoming a cop was something he'd been planning for some time while he played baseball. He'd slowly obtained his college degree in Criminal Justice. Judy had known about his goal and had been supportive while he worked towards his degree. "If it's what you want to do" is what she would always say. Canaugh had told her what he'd learned about certain drawbacks to the job. The job had risks of injury and death, which were obvious and didn't need discussion. A less obvious drawback were the hours involved. Cops worked in shifts, which meant that some of the time he'd be gone in the evenings, and some of the time he'd be gone all night. When Canaugh discussed that with her, she'd wagged her head from side to side as if weighing the pros and cons, and then she'd say, "Are you going to be gone for six months at a time?", indicating that she'd already experienced his absences, and that periods of time when he would be gone overnight would be tolerable. He told her that a good bit of the time he'd be short on sleep, and not at his best. He told her what he'd heard about job stress and how it could damage guys. He told her about a phrase he'd heard repeatedly about being a cop—"It's 90 per cent boredom and ten per cent terror." She'd reply, with a hint of sarcasm, "You're not going to be in the Army, Canaugh. You can quit."

Canaugh liked being a cop in Minneapolis. Being a cop was more than just a job, he figured. The guys he saw working in City Hall in the tax assessors' office had a job. When he played baseball, playing baseball wasn't a job. A job was something he did in the offseason. No, being a cop was more like being a ballplayer, Canaugh thought. It was a calling, a vocation. It had certain similarities. Not everyone could do it. You had to have minimum physical and mental abilities. Most everyone around had an emotional attachment to the job. You wore a uniform. The job had discipline, rituals, unwritten rules. It was a job for men, although that was starting to change. Being a cop meant being in a brotherhood of mutual affection and respect. That brotherhood extended not just to officers in the Minneapolis Police Department, but to all cops he encountered everywhere.

Canaugh and Judy had always lived in St. Paul since they got married. Minneapolis didn't require that its cops live in the city, so they continued to live in St. Paul. They liked St. Paul. Its picturesque neighborhoods had a leafy gracefulness. Very few of its streets had curbs and gutters, which reminded the couple of their small-town life in Albany and St. James. Canaugh tolerated the wise guys on the Minneapolis force when they teased that St. Paul was Minneapolis' nicest suburb. Once he had been on the force for a while, he and Judy began house-hunting. With their two incomes, they knew that they could qualify for a mortgage. After a few months of looking, they found a two-bedroom bungalow they liked on Linwood Avenue, about six blocks south of Grand. The neighborhood had houses of various sizes built mostly in the 1920's, and some smaller brick apartment buildings. The anchor for the neighborhood was Randolph Heights Elementary School, which assured that the neighborhood would always be attractive to young families. Canaugh was bemused that the neighborhood for miles around was flat as a pool table, but the school had the word "Heights" in its name.

Canaugh and Judy had more income and more time spent together than ever before. They embraced their new routine of work, relaxation, and weekends with each other. They each looked forward to better days ahead.

CHAPTER 11

June 1960

After a few years of trying to get pregnant with no results, Judy told Canaugh that it was time to involve a doctor. Judy had done the research to find a recommended clinic and doctor. Canaugh had little enthusiasm for involving medical doctors in the details of the couple's sex life, but he wanted to make Judy happy. The couple was nervous for days prior to the scheduled appointment. They each took a day off work. The Mayo Clinic is in Rochester, about 90 miles south of St. Paul. It's in a building with a somewhat severe light gray stone exterior that quite firmly announces to the world "We are serious people doing important things."

They drove down to Rochester, leaving St. Paul as the sun was rising. Canaugh and Judy held hands as they walked from the parking ramp into the lobby of the building, something they didn't usually do in public, at least not in the morning. The doctor was a few minutes late for the meeting, held in the doctor's office, rather than an exam room. Canaugh noticed that Judy smiled a lot while they waited, but her hands were shaking, a nervousness he hadn't seen since their wedding day. The doctor came in and introduced himself. Dr. Donald Murphy was in his 50's, wearing a gray tweed suit. He had a kind and wise face. He took charge right away and asked questions about their efforts to get pregnant, and the medical history for each of them. He used the word "intercourse" a lot, but in a very clinical fashion which put them at ease. He advised that some testing for each of them was the next step, and because they were from out of town, they should use the opportunity of their visit to get as much done as possible. He pressed a button on the phone and soon two nurses appeared. The doctor gave the nurses each a form with boxes checked, and Judy and Canaugh followed the two nurses out into the hallway. The older nurse told Canaugh, "Come with me. Your wife will be going with the other nurse." Canaugh looked over his shoulder at Judy. Though he intended to smile, all he did was lift his eyebrows.

The nurse was older than Canaugh, and her experience showed in her calm and business-like demeanor. She led him into a small room and closed the door. She handed him a small plastic jar with a white lid. "I need a sperm sample from you," she said. "I will presume that you know how to produce one." Canaugh almost said, *I should, I played minor league baseball*, but thought the better of it. Her face showed no trace of a smirk. "Press the red button when you wish me to return." With only a nod, she turned and left him alone in the room.

Not the time for jokes, thought Canaugh. *I'm in the Mayo Clinic*. With a bit of effort, Canaugh produced the sample, rearranged his clothes, washed his hands, and pressed the red button. He expected the nurse to check out the contents of the jar, but she took the sample without any facial expression, as normal as if he were handing her the morning newspaper. She led him to an interior lobby and told him to wait. Canaugh waited, patiently at first. After an hour and a half, he stood to stretch his legs. He realized that an exam for Judy was going to be more involved than his trip to what he'd begun to think of as "the jerk-off room".

After half an hour more, Judy appeared. "We're supposed to go to lunch and come back by 1:30." She looked pale and worried. They stopped at the information desk and asked for recommendations as to where to go for lunch. Canaugh looked over the list he was given, and his ballplayer instincts took over as to how to find a decent and affordable meal. Playing minor league baseball, he'd been in hundreds of restaurants in hundreds of towns and had an instinct as to what to look for. He ruled out restaurants with just a man's name ("Michael's) as being too expensive and formal. Restaurants with a woman's name ("Mabel's") were always possible. His eye stopped at the name "Green Parrot" and his hunch told him that it would be cheap and cheerful. "Cheap and cheerful" was the sought-after standard for minor league ballplayers when it came to restaurants. Restaurants named after birds and animals tended to be just what was needed. The first thing Judy said when they were seated in a booth was "I don't want to talk about it."

Canaugh, embarrassed, found it easy to reply, "Well, I sure don't want to talk about it either." They ordered grilled cheese sandwiches and Cokes. They found it hard to talk about anything. They were both stressed out from their morning's experience. They held hands again as they walked back to the Mayo Clinic building. Canaugh stopped at a tiny storefront called Readmore News and bought a copy of Sports Illustrated so he'd have something to do in the waiting room.

Judy was gone from 1:30 until a little after 3:00. When she returned, her face was still pale and stressed. She sat down next to Canaugh. "They want me to come back tomorrow for some more tests and to see the doctor." They conferred about whether to go home or stay overnight in Rochester. It was about two hours each way to go home and back, and Canaugh didn't want to rise in the dark for a long car trip two days in a row. He proposed that they stay in Rochester overnight. Judy agreed. They stopped at the desk again and got a list of local hotels. Canaugh, out of habit, skipped over the hotels with recognizable name brands, and settled on the Trius Hotel. The hotel was older and a bit tired, quite similar to hotels where ballplayers stayed in small cities. It wasn't until they were settled in the room that

Canaugh figured out that the hotel's name was chosen to urge potential customers to "Try Us." They each made calls to arrange to take the next day off. They had dinner out, sharing a bottle of wine to steady their nerves. Neither could sleep well, so they spent a good part of the night just holding each other. Judy didn't talk, quite unusual for her. Canaugh's instincts, reliable from years of playing ball, told him that there was a dark cloud on the horizon.

After the better part of the morning spent alone in the waiting room, Canaugh was instructed by a nurse to follow her back to the doctor's office. Judy was waiting in the office, fully dressed. She grasped Canaugh's hand tightly. Dr. Murphy came in and took a seat. He made long eye contact with each of them and managed the smallest of smiles. He leaned forward and began to speak in a low soothing voice. "We have discovered some uterine tumors in Mrs. Canaugh. We won't know if they are benign or malignant for a day or so. As to what this means for how we treat this condition, it is too early to say. I'm sure you understand that our recommendations will be dependent upon the results. I know it is pointless of me to urge you not to worry but try your best to not concern yourself until we have a full set of results. Having said that, you are free to go. Someone from our Clinic will be in touch with you with the results and to set up any additional necessary appointments." With that he nodded emphatically and rose. He shook each of their hands and left the room. Judy burst into tears and Canaugh just held her tightly. Within a few minutes Judy had composed herself sufficiently so that they could make their way through the busy ground floor lobby. Once in the car she began to cry again. Canaugh thought the best thing to do at that moment was to get home. He drove to St. Paul, a bit over the speed limit, lost in thought. Neither of them spoke.

When the call came the next afternoon that Judy's tumors were malignant, Canaugh wasn't surprised. His hunch had told him so. Whether it was because he was Irish or because he'd played a lot of baseball, he'd long ago decided that at times your luck was either running with you or it was running against you. Judy was crying and trembling. Canaugh did his best to support her. To his surprise, that only lasted less than an hour. At that point she wiped away her tears, looked him in the eye and said, "Well fuck it, Vince. We're gonna beat this." Canaugh felt joy at hearing her express a combative spirit, though he was startled to hear Judy use the f-word for the very first time. She also never made a habit of calling him "Vince", only on special occasions. He'd felt that a corner had been turned.

While in future years Canaugh could remember perfectly all the details of their first trip to Rochester and the afternoon they got the test results, the next few months were only a blur to him. They drove to Rochester and met with Dr. Murphy again, and though Canaugh did his best to focus, he found it hard to concentrate as the doctor talked in terms of "chemo" and "radiation". He was pleased that Judy was all done crying. Her chin was up, and she was in a mood to fight.

Judy took medical leave from her teaching job. Canaugh explained to his superiors his need for additional time off. Judy arranged with the Mayo Clinic to get most of her radiation treatments at Regions Hospital in St. Paul to minimize her trips to Rochester. Canaugh and Judy took regular trips through the farm fields of southern Minnesota to Rochester for exams and tests. They began to refer to it not as a trip to the Mayo Clinic, but rather as "a ride in the country." If they needed to stay overnight in Rochester, they stayed at various hotels, but never the Trius again. They both associated the Trius with bad luck.

Judy's spirits stayed upbeat even though the reports they were getting weren't always good. "We're going to be all right" she'd say to Canaugh, and he took pleasure in always hearing her refer to their situation as "we" rather than "I". He felt that she was expressing her love and regard for him when she expressed it that way. Whenever her spirits got low, Canaugh could get her to smile by repeating the uncharacteristic and somewhat embarrassing words she'd said that day upon hearing the news. "Fuck it. We're gonna beat this."

When the treatments changed to chemotherapy and her hair began to fall out, she began wearing a wig she bought at Dayton's. Canaugh made an effort to routinely compliment her on her appearance, and to reassure her that she was still attractive. It was hardly necessary for Dr. Murphy to advise the couple that having children was now out of the question. They'd accepted that outcome since their first Clinic visit, though they never spoke of it to each other. Canaugh thought that the tears would come from Judy at that moment, but they didn't. "There are alternatives, I know, and I'll always have my husband," she responded. All she did was swallow.

It was in the spring that the news got worse. Judy was dealing with days of fatigue and listlessness which she attributed to the chemo. Canaugh insisted that they go have it checked out. At this clinic visit, once the test results were in, Dr. Murphy thought it best that she check into St. Mary's Hospital. He said arrangements would be made by phone while they drove over there. It was only about six blocks. Canaugh dropped her off under the portico to wait while he parked the car. As she got out of the car, she gave him a smile and said, "We're going to be all right."

Dr. Murphy stopped by the hospital room after all the processing was done to get her checked in. Canaugh was grateful that they had put her in a single room. Dr. Murphy wore a kindly expression, but he was blunt in his message to them. "Things are not going like we'd hoped. There's some indication that the cancer has metastasized. I am going to bring in a surgeon to consult and see what's possible. I will stop in tomorrow. The staff here will give you some idea of when I'm coming." He didn't ask for questions. The doctor gave his usual professional smile and nod as he rose and left the room.

Canaugh spent the next hours holding Judy's hand while

she drifted in and out of sleep. Judy spurned the tray of food they brought her. Canaugh looked it over and he rejected it too. With Judy's approval, he left to check into the Fiksdal Motel across the street from the hospital and to find a hamburger for dinner. He stayed with Judy until she appeared to have fallen into a deep sleep. He kissed her cheek and left. He spent a restless night in his hotel bed. The next morning, he explained his situation to the desk clerk and how he didn't know if he should check out or not. The desk clerk, a well-groomed older woman, probably the owner, must have heard stories like his every day and she was sympathetic. She offered to hold his room for him until 4:00.

Canaugh stayed all day with Judy in her room. Dr. Murphy, they were told, would be by at 2:00. They weren't surprised at all that he didn't come by until a little after 3:00. This time he displayed no professional smile. His message to Canaugh sounded like a baseball coming off the barrel of a bat right at his head. "Our surgery team has declined to operate. The x-rays indicate that there are too many tumors, and the risk of not surviving surgery is too great. As always, you are invited to seek a second opinion. I'm sorry. We are going to make arrangements for you to have palliative care in St. Paul. However, there's nothing more that we think we can do in terms of medical intervention. I can only wish you the best." With that he shook Canaugh's hand and laid his hand on the back of Judy's hand and patted it as a farewell.

That is the last conversation with doctors that Canaugh remembered. What followed was a blur. There were lots of arrangements to be made. He took Judy home. He was on the phone for a day, renting a hospital bed for her, and arranging for a visiting nurse. He talked to the social worker at St. Mary's Hospital about care options. He called Judy's parents, who immediately drove to St. Paul to see her. He spent a lot of time with Judy. She was too fatigued to talk very much, so he carried the conversation. He talked about what was in the newspaper, and what was in the sports pages. He doubted that she had much interest in either subject, but he didn't want any quiet in the house. He kept the radio on to KSTP, a combination of music and chatter. He didn't want Judy to be alone. He only slept well about one out of every three nights, when he was so exhausted that he was unable to do anything else. The other nights he would stay awake, to be with his wife, aware that these were her final days, trying to imagine his future life without her.

And then she was gone. He awoke one morning and found that she had died in her sleep. He started to sob. He was alone in the house. It was his turn to swear. "Fuck it!" he shouted.

CHAPTER 12

July 1966

Judy had been gone for six years. At first Canaugh found it hard to deal with the pain and loneliness that her loss caused. He knew from his days in Albany that drinking was a way to deal with the pain. He started but then stopped when he thought of what his parents would think and then what Judy would think. In his hometown, he saw many war veterans spending too much time in the bars because it was their only way of dealing with what they'd experienced in Europe and the Pacific. As a cop and as a former ballplayer he knew that the problem with having a drinking habit is that it was a one-way street to even further loss. Canaugh decided that the best way to cope with the ache he felt when he was alone was to immerse himself in work. He wanted to stay busy. He volunteered for extra duty shifts. He took part time jobs at banks, at liquor stores, and at sporting events where extra security was needed. After a couple years he realized that he was nearing 40. He decided that life's adventure of having a wife and family had passed him by. He took a few women out on dates, but never got past the awkwardness of feeling that he still had a wife. His friends and co-workers fixed him up with women they knew, but nothing clicked. The women his age that he got to know had all been married before and he spotted their flaws. They all got compared to Judy and were found wanting. He became resigned to the fact that Judy was likely the only woman in his life that he'd ever have.

After ten years with the Minneapolis Police Department, Canaugh got promoted to Lieutenant, serving as a detective, mostly with the homicide division. Canaugh's promotion to Lieutenant was faster than normal in the MPD, but there were many reasons for that. He had a college degree. He had the prestige of having once been a professional ballplayer. He was well-regarded by his superiors and well-liked by his fellow cops. He'd done all the little things cops do to get noticed and chosen for advancement. He demonstrated self-discipline; he was punctual, stayed in good physical shape, and kept his cool under pressure. He was known for keeping quiet, particularly when circumstances benefitted other cops from his having done so. When his positive traits were recited to him as part of his annual fitness review, Canaugh recognized that his experiences in baseball most likely were responsible for the habits that made him a good cop.

Once he was promoted to detective, his interpersonal skills caused him to excel in the job. Everyone said that he was a "good listener". Canaugh didn't know if that was true or not, but he'd learned that the best way to listen to someone was to consciously not say anything. He recalled the nuns in Albany telling their students to "keep their ears open and their mouth shut." Canaugh may not have seen the wisdom in that advice as a youngster, but he did as an adult.

In talking to a suspect, a witness, or anyone from whom he needed information, Canaugh learned that the most effective way to get information was to smile a lot, nod a lot, and if he said anything at all, he only said the word "Oh" which caused most people to keep talking. Canaugh learned that it was just as important to pay attention to not only what someone said, but how they said it. From playing cards for small stakes in all the down time in minor league baseball, he'd learned important "tells", indications as to what people were thinking as they studied their cards and planned their strategy. Finding someone's "tells" couldn't be done immediately in a conversation, but if Canaugh could keep a person talking the "tells" would start to show. Most cops took notes while talking to someone. Canaugh decided that the most important thing to do was to keep his eyes on the face of the person he was talking to, and to memorize all the details of the conversation. He developed the ability to replay it all later, as if he had a mental tape recorder, when he was ready to sort out the information and make notes for the file. He made a practice of not taking any notes while talking to someone but being careful to remember all that got said while he looked for tells on the part of the talker. Part of his ability to listen to people was to also think about what people weren't saying. When someone didn't bring up an obvious topic, it usually was a sign to Canaugh that the person didn't want to discuss something, so Canaugh made a point of following up about what didn't get said.

From his training and from his experiences in life Canaugh had come to a few conclusions about dealing with people. First, most people are hard-wired to tell the truth. It comes from how people are socialized in their families and their schools. That didn't mean that people always told the truth, but it did mean that people would unintentionally disclose when they weren't telling the truth. Canaugh got introduced to the basics of "body language" in police training and was so taken by the subject that he bought books to educate himself as much as possible on the topic. Second, most people didn't know what information was important to reveal or to conceal. As a result, there was much to be gained just by having people keep talking. Canaugh would just keep waiting for the possibility that the person he was talking to would eventually spill something useful for his purposes. Third, most people, from all walks of life, got nervous when talking to cops. It caused most to lose focus, and also lose their confidence. For every interaction, Canaugh had to decide if he was better off attempting to intimidate his subject, or to get them to relax. "Kick ass or kiss ass" were the alternatives as he saw them for each human interaction, and he usually had to decide quickly. He had facial expressions to give to his subject for each of these two approaches. Canaugh paid attention to his own body language and his spacing with the person he was talking to. He mostly kept his arms by his side. Canaugh thought that when someone asking questions crossed their arms in front of their chest, it suggested that the listener was closed off and skeptical of what was being said. Someone putting both hands on their hips was usually perceived as an aggressive gesture, and Canaugh used that only when needed.

Canaugh observed that in Minnesota guys weren't comfortable standing face to face with another guy. Canaugh used that position only when it was necessary to confront someone. When he wanted to obtain someone's confidence, it was more relaxing to stand side by side, or at a 45-degree angle to his subject. Canaugh didn't touch his subject, though he was aware that it could sometimes be useful. Canaugh observed in his playing days that his teammates from the East Coast were into touching another guy when they wanted to make a point. They would lay their knuckles or fingernails on a guy's chest, and lightly tap them when they wanted to make a point. It wasn't unusual to see a New York Italian gently touch another guy on the elbow when he wanted the listener's attention, or to persuade them on a particular topic. Canaugh kept those techniques in his bag of tricks, but in Minnesota touching another guy was frowned upon in nearly all circumstances.

As a pitcher in baseball, he'd learned that success usually depended upon keeping a hitter off balance, unsure of what was coming next. Pitchers changed speeds with their pitches. They threw curveballs to surprise the batter. Asking questions as a detective, Canaugh applied those same techniques. He began to think of formulating his questions as change-ups and curveballs.

Canaugh had been assigned to important cases. The Chief left it unspoken, but he trusted Canaugh to work on the most high-profile cases and more importantly, let the Chief take the credit if the case got resolved satisfactorily. There was the murder of the heir to the supermarket fortune. There was the kidnapping for ransom of the wife of the founder and head of the brokerage firm. There was an art heist from the Minneapolis Institute of Art. There was the hold-up of a flower store that turned into a double homicide. Canaugh solved them all and stayed in the background while the Chief preened at the press conferences afterward.

After Canaugh's involvement in the prominent case of the murder and blackmail of a bank president's mistress, he was invited to lunch by Rob Whitmore, a prominent criminal defense attorney in Minneapolis. After settling on the date and time for the lunch, Whitmore indicated that it would be at the Minneapolis Club, and he added on instructions on how to handle free parking in the Club's parking ramp. *The Minneapolis Club?* thought Canaugh. *This is not merely going to be some get-acquainted session.* He'd never been there. The Minneapolis Club had been on the corner of Second Avenue and Eighth Street in downtown Minneapolis, close to all the large banks and office towers. It was a three-story building made of dark brick with leaded windows, covered with ivy vines, built in the shape of a fort. Canaugh had always thought that its appearance sent the message that it served to protect the haves from the have-nots. At noon, men in nice suits could be seen entering the building in pairs for lunch. It was a fortress of male power. For most of its existence, women had to use the back door to enter the premises.

Canaugh wore his nicest suit, purchased at Liemandt's, a classy men's store on Nicollet Avenue. This navy wool suit was his only suit not bought at Sears. Like many Minnesota men, he owned one special suit for "marryin' and buryin'". He arrived early at the Club, and waited in the front lobby, watching the lawyers, bankers, and brokers enter for lunch, all apparently regulars because they would call out the Club waiters and other employees by their first names, faking a chummy friendship with the working class. Canaugh expected to be meeting only Whitmore, but Whitmore arrived accompanied by two of his partners. All three of the lawyers exhibited a forced cheerfulness with Canaugh as they escorted him into the dark oak dining room. Canaugh's instincts were heightened. Something was up.

The lawyers spent little time looking at the menu, obviously aware of its contents and ready to order their favorite lunches. Once they placed their orders, accompanied by a bit of bantering with their waiter they addressed as "Raul", Whitmore got right to the point. He explained that they were a growing law firm and had met some financial success. Whitmore was in the papers with some regularity, handling high-profile criminal defense cases. His prominence boosted the firm's other line of business, which was representing plaintiffs in personal injury cases. "We make our real money on the personal injury side," said Whitmore. "Most criminals don't have a pot to pee in, but it gets me, it gets the firm, on the front page once a month, particularly if the jury comes back with an acquittal. That gets the phone ringing with personal injury cases. There's a lot of small personal injury cases out there. Bar fights, people slipping and falling in supermarkets, low-speed intersection collisions. We don't want those, particularly. We want cases that are, well, juicy." Canaugh understood right away that "juicy" to these attorneys meant having sizable fees result from a one-third contingent fee basis.

Whitmore got to the pitch. "We have a need for a first-rate investigator. We can use one on the criminal side, and we can also use one on the personal injury side. We think our business is about to blow up. Attorneys have been allowed to advertise for some time now, but most have been too timid to do much. What you see so far is amateurish and low budget." He scoffed. "Print ads in shoppers. Quarter-page ads in the Yellow Pages. We've been talking to an ad agency. What we have in mind is starting with radio, and soon TV. A six or seven figure ad buy, we think, we hope, will generate a lot of cases. Our goal is to be the leader in advertising in the Minnesota market for PI cases. For our part, assuming we're right on the ads generating cases, we have to be ready to capably handle the cases that come in. That's where you come in."

The lunches arrived and the men took a break to eat lunch hurriedly. They made small talk about other people in the room, pointing out prominent business leaders to Canaugh. After finishing his BLT, Whitmore continued. "We have a network of cops who are 'spotters' for us. They make us aware of accident cases and they promote our firm when they talk with people who've been injured. In turn, we take care of them." Whitmore hurried on, hoping that Canaugh wouldn't ask questions about how Minneapolis cops got compensated for referring accident cases to the law firm. He'd heard rumors when he was on the force of cops getting new refrigerators and even motorcycles from law firms.

"Our guys say that you're one of the best detectives on the force." Whitmore paused, realizing that he was on a mission of persuasion and had perhaps understated the remark. He continued, "The best detective on the force. We also know what you get paid. Our guys tell us that, too. So, here's what we have in mind. You come to work for us as our private investigator. You'll work for me on criminal cases, and you'll also work on the PI cases for my partners here." Whitmore proposed a salary figure, about fifty per cent higher than Canaugh was making working for the MPD. "And," Whitmore continued, "our employees get year-end bonuses, based on the profitability of the firm. I know you'll keep our confidences, but our average non-attorney bonus last year was over ten grand." Canaugh, surprised by this development, started thinking for the first time about the possibility of leaving the force as Whitmore kept talking about a car allowance and health insurance. "Here's what we'd like to do.

If this is something you'd consider, call me and arrange a time to stop by our offices and pick up a written offer. You can look over our offices and see where your office would be. You'll get to meet some others at our firm."

Canaugh decided that the whole presentation was smooth, and he understood why Whitmore had a reputation of persuading juries to do what he wanted. All he chose to say was, "I will think it over. I'll call you in the next day or two."

Canaugh spent a restless night, and the next day made an appointment to see the Chief. He told the Chief about the offer and that he was considering accepting it. "Oh, don't do it," said the Chief. "You could be the Chief here someday. Have my job."

"Deal with the Mayor and the City Council and that whole political thing? Deal with the reporters and be on TV? No thanks." As Canaugh talked, he realized that he had no upside staying with the MPD. He spent one more restless night and then called Whitmore to stop by the firm for a visit. Within the month, Canaugh turned in his resignation from the police force and went to work as a private investigator.

BOOK II

CHAPTER 13

March 1994

Canaugh considered himself retired as of March 1st; a date circled on his calendar. There was no ceremony. When you're no one's employee, there is no luncheon, no gushy insincere sentiments spoken, no watch, plaque, or other tokens handed over. Canaugh had notified Social Security and the police pension offices that he'd elected retirement and was applying for his benefits. Canaugh had sold his house, with a closing date set soon. He no longer wanted a house for two reasons. One, his goal was to shed himself of all responsibilities. He imagined, though he had no definite plan, that in retirement he might on short notice lock his front door and go to Florida for fishing and to watching ballgames. Canaugh's retirement was not thought out in any detail. His thoughts on the subject were somewhat abstract. He sought a ridding of perceived weight followed by a hoped-for feeling of lightness and spontaneity. All of the stresses he'd experienced caused by his witnessing the defects in the human nature of others, a career of solving crimes, later accompanied by a duty of caretaking for his wealthy patrons had mostly exhausted his optimistic good nature. While working, he'd imagined that doing nothing would be appealing and that the prospect of spending his days without responsibilities would buoy his spirits.

His second reason was that the house contained too many memories of the best part of his life, his life with Judy, which had been taken from him. The changes she'd made when they'd moved in, after thirty plus years without her, now seemed gloomy. Living in a free-standing house was too quiet, particularly in the Minnesota winters when all his neighbors were shut up in theirs. An apartment was what he'd needed, Canaugh decided. Nothing to maintain or worry about. A few years ago, he'd spotted an apartment building on Portland Avenue in St. Paul. He would cruise by it from time to time in spare moments to look over the place. It was a dark brick U-shaped building, three stories high, unusual for a building that age because each apartment had small wrought iron balconies accessible by French doors. The center of the building was set back from the street and overlooked a small courtyard. An iron gate was part of a chest-high lacquered iron fence across the front of the building, which made the building look secure but dignified in an East Coast sort of way. The building was on a block containing a few free-standing houses, several more older apartment buildings, and a Unitarian Church. Canaugh didn't know much about Unitarians. He'd been told that they didn't believe in anything, and so he was puzzled as to why they went to church at all. Maybe if he lived nearby, he would attend church and possibly join the wholesome people he saw coming every Sunday morning. He wasn't sure he believed in anything at this point in his life, and so perhaps he could join others in not believing anything. He'd long ago decided that he no longer believed what he'd been taught as a boy at St. Anthony's Catholic Church in Albany.

A year or two before he retired, Canaugh had contacted the apartment building's management company and asked to be put on a waiting list for an apartment in the middle section of the building, upper-floor and south-facing. Told that the apartments in the building don't turn over that often he'd replied, "I can wait." He did get a call one day to let him know that a third-floor apartment overlooking the courtyard would become available. Canaugh arranged a tour of the one-bedroom apartment for the same day. It was nothing fancy inside; the rent was tolerable, so he thought that it fell in the category of "good enough". He told the caretaker he'd take it. At the time he visualized how he might spend the nice days of the year sitting on the balcony, enjoying the sun while he read or listened to ball games on the radio.

Canaugh moved into his apartment. It had been preceded by a difficult process of sorting out his belongings, deciding what things should be discarded now and what things he would hold onto for the time being. At age 64, sorting before moving is a slow-motion review of one's life, artifact by artifact. Desk drawers, closets, and boxes in the attic all held the potential for both joy and pain in the memories revived for Canaugh. As Canaugh was forced to review the successive chapters of his life (student, ballplayer, husband, cop, private investigator) he didn't like the descending dark feeling that possibly the best days of his life were now behind him. When Canaugh tired of the process, which feeling seemed to come earlier and earlier each day that he worked at it, he wished someone else could do it, but at the same time realized that there was no one else who could ably perform the task. Eventually, he gave up and decided to box everything up and send it along with the furniture, knowing that all the boxes could possibly fill up the living room in his one-bedroom apartment. He'd hired movers from a classified ad he saw in the neighborhood shopper, realizing that hiring the budget movers involved some risk. When the guy who owned the truck stopped by to size up Canaugh's situation he gave two estimates—one for cash and a higher one by a check. Canaugh agreed on the cash price.

Moving day was an aggravation for Canaugh. It snowed all day, which created complications. After watching his movers work for the first hour, Canaugh thought to himself, *I've definitely hired the B Team*. He did more of the work than he'd planned on, but it seemed necessary to get the job done in a day. Sitting in his new apartment in the dusk at day's end, Canaugh was so tired he couldn't get out of his chair for hours.

Canaugh spent the next week doing more sorting and putting things away, invigorated by the hopeful prospect of a new life. March in Minnesota was too cold and uncertain to spend any time on his balcony. April, usually the month of guaranteed heartbreak in Minnesota when it comes to weather, was rainy and windy. The Twins season had started, so he listened to their day games on the radio as he unpacked and settled into the apartment. At night he watched them on television.

Canaugh was disappointed after the first month or so of retirement. The joyful feeling of release he'd anticipated never happened, though he didn't know why. The weather didn't permit much in the way of outdoor activities. Out of habit he worked out daily at the YMCA to stay in shape. Some days he couldn't even take a walk outdoors. The fishing season didn't start until the middle of May. Canaugh lined up lunch with friends a few times. They were enjoyable, but Canaugh came to realize that a good many of his friends and acquaintances were related to his work, and the people he was meeting wanted to talk mostly about their work. One rainy day, Canaugh caught himself studying the "Help Wanted" classified ads in the papers. At that moment, he realized that he was bored and needed something to do.

A day or two later, he received a call from a woman who identified herself as the administrative assistant to Ira Thorpe, General Manager of the Minnesota Twins. She had a British accent which made her sound important. She asked if Canaugh would be interested in meeting with Mr. Thorpe to discuss "a professional engagement" for the Twins. He agreed that he was, and an appointment was set for the next day at Mr. Thorpe's office. She gave him basic instructions on how to find the Twins front offices but said nothing more. Canaugh felt sheepish that he'd said "yes" so quickly, even though a few months ago he couldn't wait to end his working days. "Maybe they want me to pitch," he said whimsically out loud to no one, starting his windup, careful not to hit his hand on the stacks of boxes in his apartment.

CHAPTER 14

May 1994

Canaugh appeared exactly as scheduled for his appointment with Ira Thorp, the General Manager for the Twins. Canaugh made it a habit as a cop and then as a private investigator to show up on time. "Not five minutes early and not five minutes late" was his personal rule, perhaps conditioned by the importance of being on time (or getting fined) in professional baseball at all levels. The entrance to the executive offices of the Minnesota Twins were on the west side of the Hubert H. Humphrey Metrodome, at street level. The box office took up much of the lobby. There was a small hallway that led off the lobby, monitored by a receptionist. Other than the glass panel doors to the street, there were no windows visible from the lobby in the executive offices. The office walls were all painted light gray with terrazzo floors. The whole atmosphere reminded Canaugh of federal government buildings everywhere.

The receptionist was older than Canaugh, which surprised him a bit. Car dealerships usually had attractive well-dressed young women as ornaments at the reception desk. Apparently, the Crenshaw family didn't run the Twins the way they ran their car dealerships. Arthur Crenshaw had started with one Ford dealership on Lake Street in Minneapolis. He was astute enough to see that the future in post-war America lay not in being on Lake Street or University Avenue like all the other car dealers, but rather in the suburbs where the young families were moving. Plunging significantly into debt, he opened Ford dealerships first in Richfield, then Bloomington, and then the western suburbs of Minneapolis and the eastern suburbs of St. Paul.

Art Crenshaw was not a natural TV performer, but out of personal thrift he spurned hiring professional talent and appeared in his own black and white commercials, ending his thirty-second pitch by exaggeratingly punching the air with his right arm and saying, "You can afford a Crenshaw Ford." Before long, wiseacre schoolboys and comedians were repeating the punchline to mimic Art. Art didn't care about being mocked. His pitch about his cars being affordable, even though his cars were actually no more affordable than the cars offered by other Twin City dealers, hit the bullseye with striving Minnesotans who were sensing the growing prosperity of the country in the late fifties and early sixties. Many wanted to drive a new car (unlike their parents who drove used cars), but their primary concern was how they could afford it. Ford Motor Company astutely recognized that Americans wanted status at an affordable price, and so they built larger and larger models of cars. These cars had dubious engineering and reliability, but they had plenty of sheet metal and chrome on which their dealers could sell and enjoy higher profit margins, than on the tinny economy models which Ford still made for the bottom of the car-buying market. Art Crenshaw, with only a high school degree and an excellent sense of where car buyers lived and what they wanted, was slowly getting rich.

Art liked selling cars, and enjoyed everything about the car business, but his lawyer and his accountants repeatedly advised Art about the merits of diversifying into other fields. "But I don't know any other business except the car business" Art would object, but his lawyer and accountants would give him assurances. "Oh, you can learn" they would say, and they managed to add without being obvious about their self-interest "And we're here to help you." In response to their recommendations, Art relied on his exceptional ability to sense changes coming to Minnesota and the U.S. and so he agreed to buy a television station in Rochester, followed by another station in St. Cloud. He sensed that fast food franchises had great growth potential because he knew that his car buyers didn't want the inconvenience of leaving their cars very often, so he bought one at first, and then followed up by buying nine more. As these businesses generated more and more profit in the form of cash, he looked for other opportunities. He bought a half ownership in a home building business. He opened some fitness clubs. He opened hotels next to the two interstate highways that crisscrossed Minnesota. Not everything he invested in worked out, but he was right often enough to make a lot of money. By the time he was in his early sixties he was personally very wealthy. Bankers, many of whom had given him the cold shoulder in prior years when he needed money to expand his car dealerships, now sought him out as a customer. He tried to remain out of the public eye, unlike many Minnesota men who had met some success in business and took every opportunity to get into the newspapers or on television. Some wrote books to promote themselves. Crenshaw privately scoffed at his attention-seeking fellow businessmen. "What the hell are they thinking?" he'd ask others, sure that retaining one's privacy was the only route to having a normal life.

As his various business interests grew, Crenshaw came to rely heavily on his son Leon to help him manage his businesses. Leon had the benefit of the growing affluence of his family so that he was able to obtain an MBA from the Kellogg school at Northwestern after his four years at Carleton, a well-regarded liberal arts college in southern Minnesota. Leon's expensive education left him skillful at analyzing financial performance, even though he did not yet have his father's ability to foresee what might come next in the world of profit-making. Art thought that he and Leon made a good team, with complementary strengths. Art, like many in the highest circles in Minnesota business, had certain beliefs which they relied upon in making decisions. "Only deal with people you know or can be vouched for by people you trust." The people in the highest circles in Minnesota business had networks of relationships that only the most successful could join. It helped to have old family money, but if that wasn't possible, then it was important that those who'd made a lot of money adopt the habits and demeanor of the old money crowd, which included decorum, privacy, and modesty in their habits. Art knew that some of the wealthiest men in Minnesota drove Fords and Chevy's. It was part of Minnesota culture. Art had long ago given up appearing in his TV commercials, and that gaucherie on his part was by and large forgotten and forgiven as his fortune grew, so long as he shared his wealth with the right organizations (the Republican party, the Guthrie Theater, and the Minnesota Orchestra) and that he was seen regularly, joking and slapping backs in the right places (the Minneapolis Club and Woodhill Country Club.)

Art believed, in his early sixties, that he could see around the corner and know what the rest of his life would be like. He would gradually turn over management of his business interests to Leon. He had no interest in conventional retirement, but he envisioned spending more and more time in Naples, Florida with his many Minnesota acquaintances. His two daughters had given him grandchildren, and he enjoyed having a role in ensuring that they benefitted in ways large and small from his years of hard work and the resulting financial success. He wasn't very good at golf, having spent little time playing the game while he did business. Lessons helped only a little. He did like to go fishing and could imagine having a boat someday on the Gulf of Mexico. He had a general concept of simultaneously "taking it easy" and still maintaining interest in his many businesses and looking at opportunities that came his way, even though he couldn't begin to sort out how he would handle that sizable contradiction.

For many reasons, when Leon returned from playing golf at his country club one afternoon with a report that the Minnesota Twins were going to be put up for sale, Art was negative about pursuing the subject. Owning a professional sports team, it was true, was a crown for many after a successful business career, and it provided an entry into a national network of wealthy and accomplished men. However, an asset like that ended all hope of privacy. Most every fan, even the ones in the cheapest seats, even the ones with the dimmest understanding of the game, professed to know a great deal about baseball. Even worse, most everyone had opinions on all the decisions that owners made. Whether it was spending too much, spending too little, keeping a player or trading a player, every decision was met with criticism of some sort from the local newspaper columnists and the fans in the center field seats. As a successful businessman nearing the end of his career, Art didn't want that. On top of that, unlike his other businesses, major league baseball was highly regulated. Major League Baseball, the organization of team owners, had plenty of rules and all decisions were made as a body, a miniature democracy comprised of men, many with aggressive personalities and wealth greater than his own. The players had a union, which Art had never encountered before in his business careers. Employee unions were anathema to men liked Art. "I can't see how we'd be interested," Art told Leon, and he thought that would be the end of the subject.

It wasn't the end for long. Not much later, the decision of the Twins' owner to retire and sell the team was announced in the papers. The Twins owner had inherited the team from his family and had a reputation in the media for being stubborn and miserly. Speculation broke out that the Twins might be purchased by out-of-town interests and moved to another city, which created a furor in the media, and consequently, among the members of the general public. Business and political leaders began an energetic effort to find a local purchaser for the Twins, and so Art and Leon began to get phone calls on the subject. No one was stepping forward. After a pleading call from the governor, Art called in Leon and said, "Let's take another look at this situation. Do your usual financial analysis and let me know if you see anything worthwhile."

Art may not have seen any attraction in owning the Twins, but his son Leon did, even before he signed the necessary confidentiality agreements which allowed him to take a look at the Twins books. Though Art shunned the spotlight, Leon craved it. In a metropolitan area with no celebrities, other than the people who read the news on the local channels and a small group of professional athletes, Leon could see that owning the Twins would vault him into public life, and the benefits that come with that status. Further, the Twins, as a privately owned company, did not have to disclose its financial records to any governmental agency. This allowed the previous owner ample leeway to cynically claim lack of profitability and even poverty when faced with a financial obligation (such as giving a deserving player a better contract or leasing a stadium, whether in Minnesota or the Twins spring training site in Florida.)

Leon liked what he saw after spending a couple days examining the books. The previous owner had, using his own brand of intransigence, negotiated a lease for minimal cost in the Metrodome. The Metrodome was the result of certain Twin City boosters and business leaders to build an indoor football stadium to keep the Vikings from leaving Minnesota, which would relegate Minnesota to the dreaded status of becoming a city without amenities deemed desirable by a citizenry with aspirations. "We don't want to become a cold Omaha" said a leading politician, and there were many who marched to that drumbeat in persuading the legislature in St. Paul to provide financing for a football stadium. Having the Twins play in the indoor stadium was always an afterthought. The Twins owner stayed quiet and remained mostly unavailable when the issue of the Twins financial contribution to the stadium was discussed. One Tribune columnist said it best when he described the Twins' owner as having "the instincts of a French peasant." The owner had pretended not to hear and then later not to comprehend how he might benefit from the new stadium urged by rabid football fans. Like a French peasant, he would shrug, say nothing, and wait, which turned out to be an effective negotiating tactic. Leon realized that the team's lease allowed the team to play in the Metrodome, as he told his father, "For peanuts and crackerjack".

After Leon was done with his preliminary review of the books, Art gave approval to involve his accountants and lawyers, but on condition that his interest remain secret. He didn't want to be railroaded into a situation of having to buy the team because the media and the public had developed an expectation that he would. "Be careful. Pissed off people won't buy Fords from us," he explained to Leon.

The attorneys and accountants studied the books and saw a business that made some money, good but not great, despite its backward-looking management. The value in owning the Twins lay not in its present state, but in its potential. There was much discussion about the possible increase in value if the Twins got a new stadium of its own, one built for baseball. The men assembled in the large meeting rooms of the lawyers, and accountants talked about adding value by the Twins having its own radio station, perhaps putting games only on the TV stations that Crenshaw owned, and the coming opportunities provided by cable television and cross-promotion of Crenshaw's existing businesses. Art Crenshaw was fond of the word "opportunity" and trusted his instincts about how to make money when society was on the verge of change. He gave the green light for Leon and the attorneys to begin negotiating a price. Art could see that Leon was eager to proceed with a purchase and Art trusted Leon's ability to analyze figures.

Within a month Art had agreed to purchase the Twins, despite his concerns about becoming a public figure. Stacks of papers got signed in the lawyer's office one morning, and then at a well-attended press conference, Art was announced as the new owner of the Twins.

The Metrodome had been built in the early 1980's. It had been built for cold-weather football and so some unconventional accommodations needed to be made to fit in a baseball field. Canaugh had visited only once to watch a game and was dismayed at what he saw. He immediately thought of a common farmer's expression heard around his hometown of Albany; "Looks like ten pounds of horse shit in a five-pound sack." To get right field to fit into the stadium, the football sideline seats in that area were built on folding risers, and when retracted for baseball they all faced eerily downward just beyond the right field fence. The playing surface had a spongy sub-surface to minimize (though not eliminate) injuries to football players. As a result, a batter could chop down on a pitch and use the trampoline-style bounce to reach first base while the infielder waited for the ball to descend. Speakers nearly as large as Buicks hung suspended from the ceiling cables over the playing field. A ball that hit a speaker and took an unpredictable carom in another direction, almost impossible to catch, was considered in play and the batter (but never the pitcher) benefitted from his freakish good fortune. Pitchers did benefit from some Plexiglas panels set atop much of the centerfield home run fence to make the distances more respectable for a major league ballpark. The outfield fence in right field was just a fabric curtain giving the field a temporary look. Fans sitting down the line on both the first base and third base sides found that their seats faced into the outfield, and therefore they needed to spend the evening with their necks twisted to watch the action in the batter's box. The oatmeal-gray Teflon fabric ceiling was supported by air pressure. The ceiling's color presented no problem for football players in their efforts to see the ball. That wasn't true in baseball because the flight of the ball would be hard to track (true at night, but especially true of day games) and so Canaugh saw a routine pop fly drop in for a hit while an outfielder signaled with his waving arms and upturned hands his distress at being unable to find the ball in flight. The official scorer called it a base hit which brought pain to Canaugh. Totally unfair, thought Canaugh, for a fluke like this to add a hit, a baserunner, and a potential run to the pitcher's statistics, by which the pitcher would be judged at year end for compensation and promotion. Canaugh that night surveyed the fans around him expecting them to be as disgusted as he was at this bizarre development, but the hometown fans seemed to find it entertaining. The last straw was when he left the ballpark. With the front doors open and the sagging roof supplying the air pressure, fans got pushed through the doors and blown out onto the sidewalk. Some girls screamed with surprise or delight. Canaugh was repulsed. If you loved the game, if you respected the game and its history, this perverted playground was disgusting. He'd never gone back to another game. His visit to the executive offices was his first return trip to the Metrodome in many years.

Canaugh waited about ten minutes before Ira Thorpe came out to greet him and lead him down the hall to a large room where the meeting would be held. Moving deeper into the bowels of the Metrodome, the offices didn't get any nicer. The walls all had the same single light gray color made sickly by fluorescent lighting. He didn't see any windows. The meeting room had nice furniture and a Navy-blue rug bearing the Twins logo. There were two men waiting in the meeting room and introductions were made. None was really needed for Art Crenshaw, who got his picture in the papers from time to time now that he'd bought the team. Leon Crenshaw was youngish and was dressed a bit preppy for a baseball front office, thought Canaugh, but he seemed friendly and business-like. Leon was a bit heavy, and his second chin partially obscured his bow tie. Thorpe had on a nice suit and had the calm confidence of one who'd worked his way up to the top of a large very-public enterprise. A young man named Lowell, undoubtedly a lowly paid intern eager to be part of big-league baseball, provided a pot of coffee on a tray with cups, and then left the room closing the door behind him.

Canaugh eyed his surroundings and said, "This looks like a good place to hide out during a tornado."

Leon responded, "This shithole of an office suite is an afterthought in a football stadium. Its only virtue is that it's cheap space."

Thorpe, sitting at the head of the table, leaned towards Canaugh. He wasn't interested in small talk. "We've asked you here today because we have a problem of..." he paused before choosing his words carefully, "significant magnitude. We need a private investigator who can work with us in the highest degree of secrecy. You come highly recommended to us by several sources including Chief Lundegard and Frank Herman over at Herman Bank. It needs to be understood right from the start that you can only share this information with the three of us in this room, and that the duty of confidentiality will be without time limit. Our lawyers have drawn up a confidentiality agreement which I will give you on the way out to review, sign, and return if you accept the engagement and before we pay you the retainer."

Canaugh spoke. "I've never been asked to sign one before. Most everyone takes my word on the subject. It's just expected in my line of work."

"We require one," responded Thorpe without smiling. "You'll see why in a minute." Canaugh looked at the two Crenshaws across the table, both of whom had grave faces.

Canaugh shrugged. "It won't be a problem."

Thorpe lowered his head towards Canaugh and continued in a quiet voice. "We think one of our players may be..." Thorpe paused to choose his words carefully again, "taking steps to affect the outcome of games. There can only be one reason. Gambling."

Canaugh just quietly nodded for a bit and then said, "Why do you need a P.I.? Isn't this a matter for the Minneapolis cops or the FBI? Or for MLB?"

"Oh, we've considered that. Here's the problem. This requires absolute secrecy while we investigate. The trouble with the Minneapolis cops is that they've got spotters in their ranks who feed the juicy stories to their pals at the Tribune. Especially a certain columnist that we don't control. We can't have that. We're not sure we trust the competence at this stage to the FBI. You saw what happened in the Piper matter. The Feebies aren't much good at anything other than bank robberies, and we still have the problem of the story getting out. That's a giant organization, headquartered in D.C. and we lose control immediately. Mr. Crenshaw is a big Republican donor and so it could easily become a political football. The MLB people are a bunch of overpaid stiffs, for the most part, a bunch of dumb-ass former players who bungle things all the time. Wait, did I say 'bungle'? The correct term is 'fuck up'."

This earthy embellishment earned a snort from both of the Crenshaws. "Yes, we are supposed to report something like this immediately, but we don't have much in the way of proof at this point. We can't make a mistake or the Player's Association will be all over us if we wrongly accuse the player involved. Those guys only know one way to respond to anything related to one of their players, which is to act like assholes."

"They do that about everything," chipped in Leon.

"Also," Thorpe continued, "the team needs a new stadium and so we have to manage relations with both the public and at the legislature that this is a respectable organization." Thorpe gave an ingratiating nod towards Art Crenshaw and added, "Which it is."

"OK, I see what you're thinking, but why me?" Canaugh asked. "I'm just one guy."

Thorpe responded, "We've chosen you carefully. Most importantly, you played the game. You know the game. You're the only one in this room that played baseball after Little League. If there's something going on, even if it's subtle, we expect that you can spot it. Also, you come highly recommended to us for your ability to keep things confidential."

Thorpe's mention of "confidential" caused Canaugh to think a moment about all the developments in his years as a "private investigator": of late-night trips to jails to bail out prominent people, of retrieving and escorting mistresses of wealthy men out of embarrassing situations, of locating and extricating wastrel children of well-to-do families. He knew of at least half a dozen incidents that would be front page news all over Minnesota the next day if he'd let anything slip.

Thorpe continued. He proposed a daily rate and an advance retainer, larger numbers than Canaugh had ever heard before for a Minnesota private investigator. "You'll have a cover as a scout for the team. It won't raise any eyebrows because of your years playing pro ball in our organization. We'll get you gate credentials and an ID. You'll get a pass to all home games and an assigned seat down front. We've got several saved for scouts, both ours and the other teams. You can travel with the team to away games if you think it's necessary. For any out-of-pocket expenses, you come directly to me and only to me. If you want to report any progress, come to me only. Make no written reports and don't even keep notes until we give you the green light to do so. Understood?"

Canaugh was silent for a moment as he took it all in. He had questions in his mind that were like bees buzzing around in his head, but he could only nod slowly. There would be time to think about possibly taking or declining the job as he considered the document they wanted him to sign. Rather than asking for time to think things over, which he knew would be viewed negatively by the client, he said, "Let me look over your document." Thorpe stepped out of the room for only a few seconds and was back with a white envelope bearing the Twins red and blue logo. Thorpe and Canaugh set a time to meet the next day to return the contract and get started, assuming Canaugh was taking the assignment. There were handshakes all around and Thorpe escorted Canaugh back to the lobby. Canaugh stepped out into the bright May sunshine, squinting after his time in the cave-like Twins' offices. For a minute, he used the large envelope he'd been given as a sun visor. Canaugh replayed the entire meeting in his head, concluding that Thorpe had given the matter great thought. As for the Crenshaws, Canaugh sized up Art as a smart, smart guy, but in the process of detaching from his business interests, and he thought Leon was in over his head on the business of big-league baseball. As Canaugh walked to his car, he said quietly as he often did in times of great stress, "Oh, Judy."

CHAPTER 15

May 1994

Canaugh had studied the five-page long agreement that Thorpe had given him. What's wrong with a handshake? thought Canaugh. Canaugh had signed very few contracts in his life, and they all seemed to bring sad memories. There had been a lot of minor league baseball contracts, but none to play in the major leagues. One to buy his house, one to sell it, one for the undertaker for Judy's funeral. Canaugh had read it three times before going to bed and he endured some restless sleep. It had terms he wasn't sure about. "Liquidated damages", "injunction", "mandatory arbitration". In the morning he made a phone call to Judge Isaac Brennan, known his whole life to everyone but his mother as "Ike". When Brennan answered he said, "Hi Ike, this is Canaugh."

"Canaugh. Whadd'ya know for sure?"

"Well, there's never been a Pope named Wally" was Canaugh's response, and he was rewarded with a chuckle from Ike. The two of them had been bantering back and forth for years, ever since they met in Brennan's courtroom at the Ramsey County Courthouse in St. Paul and started going fishing and drinking beer together. They had recognized each other right away as Irish contrarian soul brothers.

Canaugh got to the point. "I got a contract that needs to be reviewed, which is why I'm calling."

"If you don't read the papers, and I've never seen any evidence that you do, I'm a retired judge, not a lawyer. Don't know why you're calling me."

"Well, at the risk of adding to an inflated ego, and believe me I hesitate to say the following, you're the smartest lawyer I've met."

"Probably true," Ike responded, "but I also know that you don't get around much. What's the contract?"

"It's with the Twins. They want me to do an investigation."

"I see," said Ike. "Probably to figure out why they can't hit with men on base."

"No, and this part is confidential. It might be in connection with criminal conduct."

"I know, they want you to find who put together their bullpen. Anyway, if I decided to help you with the contract, are you in a position to pay me?"

"How about a fifth of Jameson's?" Canaugh offered.

"Don't lowball me" was the response. "I want a quart. Come by in an hour to my outdoor office suite."

Ike's outdoor office suite was an expansive front porch on the front of his home on Lincoln Avenue, on a block of gracious, though not very large homes. Canaugh figured that rather than driving he could walk to a liquor store on Grand Avenue, buy Ike's requested retainer, and then walk the rest of the way to Ike's house. It was a nice spring day to be enjoyed. In addition, Canaugh always felt that a long walk helped him clear his head. He arrived at Ike's house exactly one hour after their phone call and found Ike sitting on a large wicker chair on his front porch. Ike was a couple years older than Canaugh. His hair had been pure white for almost twenty years, which he wore long, over his ears, longer than any other Ramsey County District Court judge, a sign of his quietly rebellious personality. Ike was one of the judges on the Ramsey bench that the lawyers hoped they'd draw because he was smart, quick on the uptake, fair, and, in that rarest of qualities found in judges, humble. Canaugh had once asked Ike if he thought being a state court trial judge was the best use of his considerable talents. "Not really," Ike had said in a moment of candor, "but I wasn't going to kiss anyone's ass to get promoted to a higher court."

As Canaugh walked up the shady front walk at Ike's house, Ike called out, "You walked over? Didya' get behind on the car payments?" Ike smiled when he saw Canaugh's package in the brown paper wrapper. "I was going to insist on payment in advance, so I'm glad to see you brought that. You know it's not wise to extend credit to Irishmen." Ike took the envelope and began reading. Canaugh sat down on an adjoining chair and enjoyed the view from Ike's front porch. He enjoyed the birdsong and the gentle spring breeze, a welcome distraction while Ike read the contract and then re-read it. Ike's wife Marie stepped out and offered Canaugh a glass of lemonade, which he accepted. Ike didn't look up. He just said, "There'll be an extra charge for the lemonade," and kept reading.

"It's a generous amount of money, from what I know about PI pay" was the first thing that Ike said. "They are joining a long line of people that have overpaid someone of your limited abilities." Canaugh was ready with questions and Ike had answers. Liquidated damages, he explained, was fixing the amount of monetary damages that Canaugh would have to pay if he breached the confidentiality agreement. "The Twins wouldn't need a trial on the subject of damages because the damages are agreed on in advance." Canaugh explained that the amount was just about half of his assets other than his police pension. Ike explained that an injunction meant that the Twins could go into court and get an order stopping Canaugh from disclosing whatever he'd found. Mandatory arbitration meant that Canaugh couldn't ever sue the Twins. He would have to go to arbitration which is a wholly private process.

"Who does the arbitration?" asked Canaugh.

Ike smiled. "Mostly retired judges. At least judges who somehow haven't had enough of the pain humans inflict on each other, and don't have a front porch to lounge on like this one."

"How hideous," responded Canaugh. There was a minute or so of silence while Canaugh pondered what he'd just been told.

"They mean business, but who knows. The Twins big firm lawyers only know how to do things one way which is to go all out. The only contracts they seem to know how to write are one-sided ones. This could be the Twins standard format for employees in sensitive positions, though it's not clear to me how many information-sensitive positions they might have for their operation. The baseball part is very public, and the rest is just selling beer and hot dogs. But if you want the assignment and the money involved, all you have to do is keep secret whatever you find out without time limit. You have to take it to your grave, but I suspect given your line of work you've got a lot of things in that category already."

"If you want the assignment..." Ike had said, which is the part Canaugh had spent hours thinking about. He'd be paid well to watch baseball games, which would mean a lot of time in the dismal airplane hangar that was the Metrodome. He was to find out if a player was possibly fixing games, like the Chicago Black Sox scandal from 1919. The more Canaugh had read about that chapter in baseball history, the more he sympathized with the players. Major league players back then got paid like minor league players in the modern era. No benefits. The amounts involved weren't great, and the players accused actually had respectable performances in the series as measured by their statistics. It was the newspapers of that era who had savaged the players. The coverage was all very one-sided.

Still, Canaugh was bothered by anyone who didn't respect

the purity of the game. Despite all the long bus rides, the stays in tired and smelly run-down motels, and the uneven ability and sometimes bizarre personalities of the coaches and players he'd encountered in the minors, he respected the game. From the time the starting pitcher started his wind-up against the first batter until the final out, Canaugh believed that every player in the field needed to give the game both their undivided concentration and also their best possible effort. Anything less was a lack of respect for the game and all the players who'd ever played it professionally at all levels. Canaugh decided that, because he was curious, he wanted to try to find out if that was happening with the Twins. He also privately admitted to himself that he was bored with his retirement regimen.

"I think I can give this project one summer before I get back to my retirement," Canaugh told Ike. They had a listless conversation about plans to go fishing. Ike's wife stepped out of the screen door and asked, "Would you care to stay for lunch?"

"Oh, no, don't ask," Ike said in mock despair. Canaugh snorted at Ike's theatrics. "Thanks, Marie, but I need to get down to the Twins' offices to turn this in and get started. Sorry, I knew you wanted some diversion from table conversation with this guy."

Canaugh walked back home, still feeling unsure that he was making the right decision in signing the contract. He called Thorpe and made an appointment to see him early that afternoon. Though the day was getting warm, he put on a suit and tie for his meeting, being careful to choose another outfit than the one he wore yesterday.

Once again, he walked to the Metrodome, moving past the few fans in line at the box office and entering the cheerless gray lobby for the Twins front office. Thorpe came to get him at the appointed hour, and Canaugh followed him back to his office. Canaugh handed Thorpe the signed Confidentiality Agreement. Thorpe gave a glance to the signature page and then tucked it into his desk drawer. Though Thorpe had closed the door, he lowered his voice to almost a whisper to discuss Canaugh's assignment, which struck Canaugh as odd. They were a long way from the door in a windowless office.

"The player in question that we want you to watch is Frankie Montalvo." Canaugh was surprised, because Montalvo was a young pitcher, and up and coming member of the starting rotation. Canaugh was puzzled. A position player would have an opportunity to affect a game almost every day. A starting pitcher plays only once every five days. Thorpe continued, "As you probably know, last year was his rookie season and it was a good one. Very promising. This year he's had high moments and low moments. Sometimes he does things that we can't understand. 'We' being the skipper and me. The columnists at the paper attribute it to his lack of experience and lack of emotional maturity. Jesus, those guys know a lot less than they think they know, but they've got to fill column space twice a week so them missing the target and saying dumb things is understandable. Except when they write about me. Then it's not so understandable."

"What we want you to do is watch him. Be there each time he pitches. Chart his pitches. Keep track of the speeds with your gun. Keep track of the small things. How often is he shaking off pitches? Is he making smart pitches for each situation? For road games, travel with the team if Frankie is scheduled to pitch one of the first two games. If he isn't, check with me. Let me know when you think you're ready to report anything at all. It doesn't have to be a final conclusion. If you think we're wrong, and nothing's going on, that's OK. As we talked about yesterday, talk only to me, not even to the Crenshaws from this point forward. Don't talk to the manager or to any players. This is all top secret. Don't discuss things over the phone with me or anyone. Don't talk to the other scouts, other than a hello and a brushoff. When in doubt about anything, when you need anything to do your job, talk to me. Got it?"

"I got it," said Canaugh, aware of the irony that the same expression is used in baseball to signify that the play is yours alone. Thorpe produced a lanyard with an ID badge attached, an all-game pass good for a reserved seat behind home plate, a radar gun, a clipboard with the Twins logo on it, and a parking pass, though not for inside the east end of the Metrodome where the players and top executives parked, but for a nearby ramp. Thorpe explained some basics of how and where the scouts entered the stadium, and who he might see sitting with the other scouts. Finally, Thorpe produced a check contained in an envelope. He stood, indicating the meeting was over with, and shook Canaugh's hand. Canaugh left the Metrodome, his hands full, happy to be going to a ballgame that night, even if it was in the Metrodome.

CHAPTER 16

May 1994

Montalvo was not scheduled to pitch the first night of Canaugh's new job, but that was perfectly fine with Canaugh. He wanted to get used to the game setting and to practice a routine to use at ballgames when Montalvo would be pitching. Canaugh brought the radar gun and clipboard issued to him and set them down on the steps adjacent to his seat at the end of the row. Scouts got seats in the first two rows behind home plate. Because they were high-revenue seats, the whole row was not made available to scouts, just the end six seats in each row. From Canaugh's vantage point, he could get a good look at the pitcher, though it would be through the rope mesh that protected the fans from foul tips zooming back behind home plate at 90 miles per hour. Canaugh looked around in the adjacent seats and got both nods and puzzled looks from the other scouts who'd brought the same tools of the trade to the game. Some must have been employed by the Twins and some were from other major league teams using the seats that were made available as a courtesy to visiting scouts. No one knew who Canaugh was, but he looked the part of a scout. Graying short hair, a clipboard, and a radar gun would identify a guy as a scout on the payroll of some major league team. Canaugh brought several mechanical pencils which he stored in a vinyl white pocket protector. Canaugh had never used a pocket protector before, but he thought it would complete his disguise. Realizing that none of the other scouts used pocket protectors, Canaugh decided that it was theatrical overkill and decided right away to leave it at home from then on. A short sleeve shirt and cotton chino pants seemed to be the standard uniform for scouts.

Everyone who'd been a starting pitcher in professional baseball had spent a lot of time charting pitches. It was a baseball custom that the pitcher scheduled to start the next game sat in the dugout with a view of home plate and charted what pitch was thrown and what the result was. It was part of baseball's never-ending effort to collect all possible minute data so that it could quantify the performance of players. It was next to impossible to collect all the data and analyze it at the same time. Very basic information (number of balls and strikes thrown) is on the scoreboard in major league stadiums, but in minor league stadiums it was up to the charting pitcher to have that available if asked. Pitchers didn't have the job of analyzing all the information they collected. The job of evaluation, determining the probabilities and trends, fell to the manager and the coaches.

As Canaugh recalled his days beyond counting charting pitches, he wondered how in the world he would evaluate whether Frankie Montalvo was changing his performance in order to affect the outcome of the game. A position player had more opportunity to affect a game, thought Canaugh, because they came to bat 3 or 4 times a game, and they would inevitably get chances in the field to make a play or not. Pitchers didn't bat any more in the American League, which adopted the designated hitter rule in 1973. *Too late to save me from a lot of embarrassment*, thought Canaugh at the time. Like most pitchers he believed that he was a capable hitter, but because teams rarely allowed pitchers to practice hitting, his skills fell off rapidly after his high school days. Pitchers could serve up hittable balls but doing that would quickly result in a pitcher getting lifted. A frequent pattern of throwing hittable balls would get a pitcher sent to the minors at first, and eventually out of baseball.

All the data collected in baseball got used to create statistical measures of strengths and weaknesses for the players. Statistical measures themselves got evaluated regularly for their utility. Those regarding hitting were usually found to be lacking in one dimension or another, which resulted in new statistical measures being developed and relied upon. Canaugh knew from his thorough daily reading of the sports pages that teams and fans were starting to compute metrics like On-Base Percentage, Slugging Percentage, batting average with runners in scoring position, and other novel measurements for hitting.

Though different statistics got employed for batters, the measurement for pitchers stayed the same over many decades of the game, which were earned run average, strikeouts, and won-loss records. Canaugh thought that won-loss records were the least reliable indicator, because winning ball games depended to a great extent on the other eight players. Some pitchers got great run support and others did not, depending upon the ability of the batting order to not only hit, but hit on a timely basis to produce runs. Producing runs was out of the control of the pitcher, but nevertheless the stark end-result of winning versus losing was the largest factor in how pitchers got judged.

Producing runs was only part of the game. A pitcher, to be successful, had to have players behind him who could catch the ball or else field the ball and get it to the right teammate on a timely basis. Errors could change a game, but they didn't factor into a pitcher's won-loss record. Keeping track of errors wasn't even fair. The job was delegated to the official scorer, often an anonymous person of unknown pedigree, who tended to show favoritism to the home team's fielders by classifying errors as hits when the home team was in the field, and just the opposite when the home team was at bat. It annoyed Canaugh that the official scorer's tendency to give a break to the hometown fielders penalized pitchers because hits and earned runs got charged against the pitcher's performance. The same bias was encountered when his team was on the road. The local team was credited by the hometown Official Scorer with undeserved hits, which outcome, of all the players, reflected only on the pitcher's count of hits surrendered and earned run average.

Despite baseball's unique efforts to collect data and quantify performance in detail, in Canaugh's experience the statistics could get often set aside by managers when it came time to make a strategy decision like using a pinch hitter, yanking a pitcher, intentionally walking a batter, or changing the line-up card. Managers relied on other factors beyond logic, which had a variety of names like "intuition", "hunch", or "gut instinct." Canaugh came to realize over the years that they were just guesses, pure and simple. Despite all the data collection in baseball, no one kept track of how successful a manager's guesses were. What they'd find, Canaugh decided, was that there was no such thing as an ability to make the right guesses consistently. Some managers were lucky and got a reputation as having "good baseball instincts." *What a crock*, thought Canaugh. *All they're entitled to is a reputation for being lucky*.

"George Halas was honest enough to admit it," Canaugh used to tell teammates when the subject came up. "He'd always say 'I'd rather be lucky than good.'" Managers who guessed wrong had an all-purpose bromide they could rely on, which was to say "That's baseball" which would deflect blame from them.

Managers would do something similar in evaluating talent. It was human nature, Canaugh decided, that most managers would like some of their players and dislike some others. Over time, the managers that Canaugh came to prefer were old crusty types who didn't appear to like any of their players. For some of these curmudgeons, being disagreeable to everyone was just an inseparable part of their personality. For a few, Canaugh figured that it was tactical on their part, for the only way to remain objective in evaluating players in their dugout was to not get close to anyone.

The manager he valued the most was Doc Anderson, his manager for one summer in Big Spring, Texas. Leonard "Doc" Anderson was 70, a baseball lifer with a fondness for cigarettes and a habit of having epic coughing spells in the dugout and locker room. Doc's skin was all ruddy wrinkles, a product of having spent a lifetime of summer days outdoors. He had thinning white hair, and a lower lip that tended to hang open. Doc had made it to the big leagues for one season as a catcher with the Cubs. Before then, he'd spent seven years in the minors and after his summer of glory with the Cubs (though mostly as a bullpen catcher or being used when the game had been decided) he returned to the minors to stay. Doc's fatal flaw as a player was that he couldn't hit well enough to stick in the majors. However, over the years he'd developed an excellent sense for how to handle pitchers. He understood that once pitchers had the physical ability to make it to the double-A level and higher, a big part of success lay in the mental side of playing baseball. Issues like confidence, maturity, self-control, and humility were characteristics he paid attention to as things to develop in the young men entrusted to him. He had an extensive vocabulary, and a great understanding of psychology that he'd learned from extensive reading.

Canaugh's first game playing for Doc was memorable. With two men on base, Canaugh shook off the catcher's signs, thinking that he would try a new pitch he'd been working on in a clutch situation. The batter put the ball over the home run fence. Doc came out to the mound. He didn't make eye contact with Canaugh at first. Rather, he looked at third base and then he looked at first base, before finally looking Canaugh in the eye. Without much of any expression on his face he asked in his raspy voice, "Hey 54, what the heck was that pitch?"

Canaugh understood Doc's displeasure with him by being called by his number and not his name. "A change," he replied.

Doc spit on the ground and said, "If you throw that pitch again, you're gonna' be on the next bus out of here." And then he turned and headed back to the dugout. Canaugh responded by striking out the next two batters.

As the season went on, Canaugh kept his distance from Doc, although Doc never got hostile with Canaugh again. Doc was from Mason City, Iowa, and seemed to treat Canaugh better as time went on. Perhaps, Canaugh thought, it was because Doc had grown up so close to Iowa's border with Minnesota. Canaugh had noticed over time, as players came and went, that players from the same state seemed to become pals with each other. Perhaps it was because Canaugh had some college and was an avid reader like Doc, which merited a little better treatment from Doc. Doc didn't treat all his pitchers alike. He treated them as individuals to get the best out of each player. Although Doc had specific and highly useful teaching points for his pitchers, he had life lessons for all his players, which he forcefully made in the locker room and dugout, or sometimes in one-on-one conversations. Doc's statements were not the cliché's often seen in locker rooms about the going getting tough. His exhortations were his alone. His cardinal principle, which he repeated so often that some of the players would silently mouth the conclusion along with him, was this: "Whether it's this game or anything you do on this earth, there are many reasons you will fail, some beyond your control, but the only truly shameful reason for failing is a lack of effort."

There were some old-timey sayings he used with great frequency. "It's what you do when nobody's looking that matters." "It's locks that keep honest people honest." "If you don't make decisions, other people will make them for you."

Some were darkly comical: "Better to have been born dead than to be called out looking at a third strike."

Some were so enigmatic that the players didn't understand them and could only wonder: "You will find that your greatest weakness and your greatest strength are the same thing."

Doc never used profanity, quite uncommon in the baseball coaching profession. It wasn't that he was religious; he wasn't. Rather, as Canaugh recalled a teammate telling him, "He has no need for profanity with all the words he knows." Doc's favorite word seemed to be "spaghetti." He'd yell at the umps "You're totally full of spaghetti" or "What a bunch of spaghetti." When telling stories, he'd use the expression "That's when the spaghetti hit the fan."

Doc's frequent sayings were not beyond ridicule by the players who'd heard them frequently. One night in a bar, Canaugh and several players had gathered for some pitchers of beer. One guy returned from the men's room and said, "Someone wrote on the walls in there 'A man without God is like a fish without a bicycle.'" Someone else said, "I think Doc wrote that," and there was convulsive laughter. Others started offering hilarious variations on Doc's many sayings, each getting a big laugh. "It's cops that keep honest people honest." Another was "It's what you steal when nobody's looking that matters." The examples the players came up with soon wandered into the absurd. "In life you may come to a fork in the road, but somehow you'll never come to a spoon in the road."

Doc had a standard response to either players or reporters to certain questions he'd heard repeatedly. As to why he was still in baseball after 50 years he'd say, "Because I'm no good at golf." As to why he never married he'd say, "You're not going to meet many good women playing ball. I'll have to meet one after I'm done with the game. I'm not done with the game."

Canaugh's reverie about his summer with Doc ended with the snap of the first pitch hitting the catcher's mitt. Canaugh got busy with his charting. He decided it wasn't exactly like riding a bicycle; it had been almost forty years since he'd last worked a pitch chart and he was slow and rusty. The radar gun hadn't come with an instruction booklet so Canaugh had to spend some time learning how to operate it, concerned that his clumsiness would be noticed by the other scouts. Charting pitches and operating the gun were difficult, so he was glad that he'd decided on a practice game. Canaugh left after eight innings. He was tired and had yet to determine how he could evaluate whether a pitcher was giving his best effort or not. He decided that was something he would try to figure out the next day at home, and not in a stadium. He left the Metrodome by the front door, walking past a plastic-pail drummer and a bearded fiddler setting up outside to play for tips from the departing crowd.

CHAPTER 17

May 1994

Influencing the outcome. Canaugh pondered Thorpe's words in his mind as he sat at his dining table, which doubled as his desk. Thorpe's choice of words seemed quite vague to Canaugh. A pitcher could influence the outcome of a game by serving up hittable pitches to batters but there were certainly limits to that strategy. If a pitcher served up a meatball to a batter with runners on base in the major leagues, the ball would be headed over the fence to where the Cub Scouts and the Rotarians on their summer outings sit. Every batter in the majors was capable of hitting a home run on a fat pitch. OK, not every batter, Canaugh decided. Most pitchers couldn't hit one but perhaps a few could. Most pitchers were good athletes, and most were good hitters in high school and early in their career. However, pitchers didn't spend any time taking batting practice once they got to professional baseball at any level, and as a result their batting skills atrophied down to nothing, with one or two exceptions. In the American League, pitchers never batted at all, due to the designated hitter rule. In the National League, pitchers batted but most were considered automatic outs.

A pitcher risked career damage by allowing runs. Pitchers weren't like ice skaters or Olympic divers. They weren't evaluated on their looks or their form. They were evaluated by their statistics, an unforgiving method of determining the worth of any pitcher. Allowing hits that led to runs would immediately affect a pitcher's Earned Run Average. The ERA was an important statistic, more important to baseball management than a pitcher's won-loss record. On teams without good hitters or with a mediocre or losing record (which would be about half the teams in any league), the ERA was the most important statistic for a pitcher.

In addition to statistics, there were intangibles. A pitcher had to earn the confidence of the team manager that he could capably get outs in any situation. Trust could be damaged if there was any suspicion that a pitcher was not doing his best all the time.

Canaugh had asked for and obtained a complete copy of Montalvo's personnel file, which was given to him by Thorpe in a red file jacket marked "Confidential—Return to Ian Thorpe Only". Canaugh assumed that it was complete, but he had no way of knowing. Canaugh spread the documents out on his dining room table. Montalvo had succeeded at every level that he'd pitched. Canaugh couldn't help comparing Montalvo's statistics to his own. Montalvo's learning curve was much faster than Canaugh's. Canaugh's experience had been typical for pitchers. With each new team he struggled a bit at first, and then with time and experience showed some competence. Montalvo's was different. He succeeded right away and had decent numbers with each of his stops on the way up the ladder. Unlike Canaugh, Montalvo did just as well in triple-A as he had in double-A ball, a statistic that gets you noticed in the front office of major league clubs.

Montalvo was selected at spring training in 1993 to come north with the team as a starter, an unusual outcome for someone only 21 years of age with just 3 years in the minors. His first year with the Twins he had a record of 7-5, with an ERA of 4.21. Canaugh dug down to see the dates he'd pitched and the outcomes. Montalvo had won 4 of his last 5 starts, mostly in September. Canaugh spent time with his calculator to determine Montalvo's ERA for the last five games. He made the calculation twice because he was unsure the first time that he saw the result. When he got the same result the second time, he whistled. It was 2.26, better than the season average for any pitcher on the Twins' staff, starter or reliever. Canaugh took into account that September was a bit different in the majors because teams were allowed to expand their rosters and so they called up a lot of minor league prospects. If the team was no longer in contention for a playoff spot, teams put their bench players and minor leaguers in games to see how well they would perform. September pitching statistics were therefore not perfectly reliable, but still trustworthy for the most part. There was no doubt, Canaugh concluded, that Montalvo was a pitcher of considerable ability and promise. Montalvo, in his second season in the majors, was a bargain for the Twins. He was the lowest paid pitcher on the staff and had this season and next season to go on his rookie contract at that level.

But Canaugh still had two important questions. The first was why would someone with the future potential of Montalvo get involved in cheating, if he indeed was cheating. The second was how could he cheat and not pay the price in terms of damage to his statistics. Canaugh decided that he was unlikely to discover the answer to the "why" question just by watching him pitch, and so that could be investigated later. Besides, he thought, the logical thing to do was to see if he could answer the "how" question first. If he reached the conclusion that Montalvo wasn't cheating, then it wouldn't be necessary to determine why.

Canaugh decided that he didn't know much about gambling on baseball. The casinos in Las Vegas were the only place where one could place legal sports bets. Canaugh was aware that there was lots of illegal gambling on sports. He knew from his days on the Minneapolis force that it was easy to become a bookie. From arrests made and discussed among the cops, a typical story was that some guy started taking bets among friends and then friends of friends, usually on professional football, until the volume was such that the amateur bookie decided that there was enough money to be made to turn pro. It was fairly low overhead. Gambling in football was determined by the point spread; the favored team needed to win by the amount of the point spread, or else it was considered a loss. Point spreads were set at the start of the week based upon the estimation of the casino professionals as to what point spread would bring in an equal amount of money being bet on both teams. The point spreads were determined by the professionals in Vegas, adjusted during the week as the actual betting developed, and then published on the sports pages of every newspaper in America. Canaugh had always been puzzled as to why the newspapers published point spreads. As far as he could see, it was normalizing sports gambling, not just Nevada casino sports book gambling but illegal gambling in every state. For the amateur bookies turning pro, the wagers gradually expanded to include bets on college football, and then professional and college basketball. The bookies kept 10% of the total amount wagered, so it was in their interest to constantly expand the business.

The risk for the bookies in Minnesota was discovery by the authorities, local or federal, which usually meant a minimum jail term for a couple of years. Therefore, in the illicit gambling business, maintaining secrecy was a delicate balance. A bookie wanted new regular customers but sought to avoid being discovered. To keep their business going, bookies with a certain size book of business could start sharing profits with the cops or politicians. However, based upon his experience, Canaugh believed that the cops in Minneapolis and St. Paul played it straight, and so did the City Councils in both cities. He would amaze cops in other cities by telling them about the Minneapolis City Council member who got prosecuted for accepting a two-hundred-dollar bribe, even though it happened in the 1980's.

The illegal sports gambling business thrived in other cities, so a Minnesotan wanting to bet on a game wasn't limited to small-time Minnesota operations. In other Midwestern cities, like Chicago, Detroit, and Kansas City, the rumor mill on the cops' network was that gambling was tolerated because the enforcement arm of the local government was either sharing in the profits, or a decision had been made that gambling was in the nature of a public service and so long as it was kept underground and didn't lead to other forms of crime, it would be tolerated. Gambling eventually came to the attention of state governments as a profitable line of business. Cops once had to be on the alert for numbers rackets in their jurisdiction. Numbers rackets were illegal small bets which paid off when winning numbers were determined by the order of finish in horse races. Many states, whose politicians once deplored this form of gambling, took it over by sponsoring lotteries for small bettors with large payoff amounts. The state lotteries were advertised on TV as wholesome fun, with colorful commercials. There was plenty of the same type of advertising in convenience stores. The numbers rackets went out of business once the state governments took it over. The states made a lot of money. It was the same type of business that was once illegal. Canaugh shook his head when he thought about it.

American attitudes about gambling were changing. The Native American Indian tribes, whose members had been for the most part excluded from the various American routes to prosperity, asserted their right to operate low-stakes casinos on reservation lands. The tribes used multiple avenues of persuasion, including filing legal actions, using political influence, and forming alliances with those businesses and law firms who would benefit from legalizing casino gambling. Canaugh had noticed over the years the irony of those who had for years wanted to be called "Native Americans" rather than "Indians" because "Indian" was a misnomer of the early

European explorers who were seeking a route to India. When Congress authorized casino gambling, it carefully chose the term “Indian” as a line-drawing exercise. The term “Native American”, Congress had learned, included other ethnic groups who were arguably descendants of those native to America, such as Russian settlers in California and European settlers who had migrated up from Mexico. For the tribes, the benefit of making sizable amounts of tax-free cash now outweighed the indignity of being called by the name they previously objected to. Gambling, Canaugh decided, was America’s unique growth industry. It grew and grew, and it never shrank.

Canaugh decided that he knew nothing about gambling on baseball, other than he surmised that bettors would try to pick the winner of each game. Because baseball teams now could be characterized as either “haves” or “have-nots” he thought that there couldn’t be much interest in betting on baseball. He picked up his copy of the Pioneer Press and studied all the agate type in the sports pages. He found, in an obscure corner, a box called “Today’s Line” which had a list of all the games to be played. He’d seen it before but never paid much attention to it because he was repulsed by the thought of betting on baseball. Adjacent to each team there was a three-digit number that was preceded by a plus or a negative sign. Canaugh stared at the box for a while, but was unable to decipher what it meant, other than its only possible purpose was related to gambling.

He made a few calls to guys he’d met either as a cop or as private investigator who he knew liked to place bets on sports. “Help me out,” he’d say after a few minutes of polite and mostly insincere conversation about recent developments and asked his questions. He learned that betting in baseball was mainly about figuring out which team would win and by how much. The “line” in the newspaper could be interpreted as follows. The team with the negative number was the favorite. The three-digit number was missing a decimal point, which could be imagined after the first digit. The number “minus 255” (which should be read as -2.55) meant that the favored team needed to win by three to be considered the winning team for betting purposes.

What does this mean for my purposes, thought Canaugh as he stood up to pace around his apartment. Though betting on a baseball game mostly meant choosing the winning team, the run differential represented the projected point spread, just like in football betting. If a casino expert was setting the line each day, what factors would go into choosing the point spread, Canaugh pondered. The most important factor would be which team was the home team, because statistically most teams won more often at home than on the road, though there were seasons when one or two teams proved the exception rather than the rule. The second-most important factor would be who the starting pitchers were, because it was a common belief in baseball that good pitching would invariably triumph over good hitting.

The more Canaugh thought about the structure of baseball betting, the picture became less clear, rather than leading him to any insight. The margins of winning in betting were so tight that a pitcher, if he wanted to affect the outcome, would most likely be giving up the winning run by giving a batter a hittable pitch. A situation where there were men on base would likely lead to multiple runs and a certain loss. Besides a starting pitcher rarely pitched the whole game in the modern era. After six or seven innings, most starting pitchers got lifted for a relief pitcher. A relief pitcher could more likely affect the outcome of the game by throwing hittable pitches. The only situation where a starting pitcher could affect the betting line would be if the pitch would lead to one run where the betting line was between one and two runs. That would not change the game outcome from a win to a loss, but it would change the betting outcome on the favorite from a win to a loss. And that would be true only if nothing changed in the final innings when a relief pitcher was on the mound. Canaugh scratched his head. He said out loud in his empty apartment, "I don't get it. It's such a narrow circumstance that a pitcher could 'affect the outcome' without detection because that situation doesn't present itself very often. I'm just not seeing something."

CHAPTER 18

June 1994

Canaugh went to the Metrodome for the night's game against the Kansas City Royals. He exchanged the usual puzzled nods with the other scouts as he took his place at the end of the row and unpacked his gym bag containing the radar gun and clipboard. Frankie Montalvo was introduced as the starting pitcher. Canaugh had brought along his binoculars to get a close look at Montalvo as he finished his warm-up tosses before the top of the first inning. Canaugh certainly recognized what he saw. Montalvo had the "game face" of most starting pitchers, who'd had the opportunity to think about their start since they woke up in the morning. He had a light sheen of perspiration from his pre-game warm-up. His nostrils were flaring as he took deep breaths while he dealt with his nervousness. Canaugh recalled visiting the paddock at Canterbury Park and how the thoroughbreds looked and acted just before they were mounted by their jockeys and led out to the track for their race. They too had a sheen of sweat, flared nostrils, and eyes staring ahead at nothing in particular. Starting pitchers and racehorses, thought Canaugh, both got absorbed the same way by the anticipation of the competition ahead. Both were thoroughbreds, Canaugh thought, who thrived on competition.

Nothing much happened in the game that struck Canaugh as curious. Montalvo had a good outing, striking out seven and limiting the Royals to two runs. It wasn't until the seventh inning, which turned out to be Montalvo's final inning, when he noticed something. Canaugh was casting his eyes around the nearby seats, mostly people-watching. He stopped when he saw an unusual-looking man sitting nearby in the front row, near the Twins dugout but just at the edge of the protective net. He wore a red Twins warm-up jacket, an original old-style Twins cap, and longish white hair. He had a scorecard on his lap, not the five-dollar kind that the Twins sold at their concession stands, but a professional kind with a spiral wire binder. At first Canaugh checked him out because he didn't look like the average Twins fan that came to the games. His age, his clothes, the fact that he seemed to be all alone rather than with a companion, all indicated that he was out of the ordinary. Canaugh, from his years as a cop and a private investigator, paid attention to things out of the ordinary. It was instinct.

The man seemed to be paying great attention to Montalvo. He seemed to be staring at the young pitcher. The man then touched his nose in what looked like a signal to Canaugh. Canaugh looked quickly at Montalvo to see if Montalvo was watching the man in the red jacket, but it was too late to tell. There was nothing out of the ordinary that Canaugh could see about Montalvo's pitch. Canaugh turned his attention back to the man again, who seemed to be busy writing on his scorecard. There was no signal of any kind for the next two pitches. Then the man touched his nose again, identical in all respects to the same signal he'd given a couple of pitches ago. Canaugh looked quickly at Montalvo, but he couldn't tell if Montalvo had seen the signal or not. Again, there was nothing unusual about the next pitch from Montalvo. Canaugh had stopped using his radar gun and making notes. He was now absorbed in what the white-haired man was doing. There was no signal for the next two pitches. The first pitch was a swinging strike for the second out.

Montalvo's second pitch went to a new batter but got fouled off behind third base which the shortstop snagged for the third out. The inning was over. The manager shook Montalvo's hand as he reached the dugout, a sure sign in professional baseball that Montalvo was done for the night and that one of the two relievers who'd been warming up in the bullpen was coming in. With Montalvo done for the night, Canaugh packed his gym bag with his belongings. As he walked to his car, he tried to make sense of what he'd just seen. He decided that he needed to come to Montalvo's next game and turn his attention to the white-haired man and Montalvo, and to keep track to see if there was anything he could measure in terms of communication between them and actual consequences. As he thought further, he decided to give the man a nickname for his purposes. From now on, he'd call him Signalman.

Montalvo's next game to pitch wasn't a home game, but rather a game against the White Sox in Chicago. Canaugh told Thorpe that he wanted to drive rather than fly on the team plane. Chicago was six hours away on the Interstate assuming that he could exceed the speed limit. Also, he hoped that with a bit of luck the Wisconsin State Patrol would overlook him. If he did get pulled over, he'd find a way to mention that he was a former cop. Canaugh didn't want to have any contact with Montalvo on the team flight, or for that matter, anyone who'd be aggressively curious about why a stranger was on the plane. Thorpe, a bit curious about Canaugh's choice, gave him the go-ahead. It was just Canaugh's well-honed instinct, when casing a situation, to remain as anonymous as possible.

In Chicago, Montalvo pitched the second game of the series. Canaugh looked carefully with his binoculars for Signalman but couldn't see him anywhere. He had the binoculars on Montalvo's face the whole game. He couldn't discern Montalvo looking at anyone between pitches except the catcher. Montalvo pitched well and by the middle innings, the Twins had a four-run lead. When Montalvo got replaced for a reliever after eight complete innings, Canaugh headed for the parking lot. Out of habit from a lifetime of necessary frugality, even though he was on the Twins' expense account, he didn't want to pay Chicago hotel prices. Also, he just didn't want to stay in a place as big and busy as Chicago. He preferred the sleepiness of St. Paul. He hit the Interstate and drove in the dark as far as Janesville, just over the Wisconsin state line, before he thought it best to stop at a Howard Johnson's for the night. He had nothing to show for his road trip to Chicago. If something fishy was going on, he hadn't figured out what it was.

For Montalvo's next start at home, Canaugh did a lot of preparation. He bought a green-tinted columnar pad at an office products store. He labeled columns to denote pitches following signals. He would keep track of what kind of pitch was thrown, the speed, whether it was a ball or strike, and the outcome for the batter. He figured out a way to cross-reference it to the game situation on the scorecard. He would do his best to both keep a scorecard and also note all the data for his columnar pad. He doubted that he could accomplish all his record keeping and use his radar gun, but he thought that he could use the stadium scoreboard's radar gun, despite his doubts about its accuracy. The stadium's scoreboard in the Metrodome, Canaugh had decided, was inaccurate on purpose. Two or three miles per hour were added for the home pitcher's tosses, and the visiting pitcher's efforts were shaded a bit low. Doing so was apparently to entertain the fans and make them feel good about the home team's hurler. Canaugh first had only suspicions about the pitch speed shown on the scoreboard based on his years of playing ball, but once he started using a radar gun his suspicions were confirmed. He'd noticed that the scouts all used their own radar guns and not the scoreboard speeds. The Twins had their own radar gun operator in a small enclosure under the seats behind home plate. The scoreboard could entertain the fans, but the team needed authenticity.

He expected that he wouldn't be able to reach any

conclusions while he was at the game. Like the time he spent as a pitcher in the dugout charting pitches for a game in process, the object was just to collect the data and not try to draw any conclusions at the same time.

Canaugh took his seat for the game. He placed his scorecard and columnar pad across his lap, one on each thigh. He put his binoculars by his left foot and his radar gun by his right foot. He thought he saw looks of amusement as well as puzzlement on the other scouts in attendance. One familiar face looked over all of Canaugh's accessories and said mockingly, "I think you forgot to bring your umbrella." Canaugh looked around. Just before the game started, he saw Signalman come down the aisle, alone, and take his seat. Canaugh watched him settle in. Signalman had his scorecard with him.

Keeping track of everything he'd planned on was a challenge for Canaugh. He had to swivel his head to look at Signalman, then look at the pitch, then the scoreboard to check out the pitch speed, and then note all the data in the notebooks on his lap. After a few innings he could feel himself getting weary from all the concentration required. As he'd planned, he didn't try to analyze the data to determine any meaning. Signalman seemed to touch his nose a bit less frequently than during the previous game, though Canaugh wasn't sure about that. Montalvo pitched a decent game, giving up six scattered hits, and walking only one batter. The Twins hitters had trouble with the Angel's pitcher so that Montalvo wasn't getting much run support. He was lifted in the sixth inning with two men on base and the score tied 1-1. Canaugh hated when that situation happened to him because the starter couldn't get the credit for being the winning pitcher, but if the relief pitchers couldn't get people out, the starter would be charged with the loss. When Montalvo headed to the dugout, Canaugh packed up his gym bag with everything he'd brought and headed up the steps.

The next morning Canaugh skipped his usual enjoyable session of coffee and the newspaper on his little balcony overlooking the courtyard. He'd slept okay, despite not seeing any patterns to Montalvo's pitching and the signals from Signalman the night before as he drove home on a warm summer night. Over the years, he'd learned to close the door on his concerns when his head hit the pillow by saying, "I'll solve that problem tomorrow."

Canaugh poured himself a second cup of coffee and spread out his charts from the night's game. He had a yellow legal pad out for making notes. He reviewed Montalvo's pitches, line by line, to try to determine any pattern. He made a graph of pitch speeds using a ruler and some graph paper. At noon, he stopped and made himself a ham sandwich. He tried every approach he could think of. By mid-afternoon he had a headache. He'd decided that he could see nothing conclusive. He called Thorpe to give him a status report. He told Thorpe that he could find nothing in his analysis after watching Montalvo pitch for three games. He then told Thorpe about Signalman, and what he'd observed about his suspicious behavior. Thorpe had little reaction. He didn't seem disappointed in what Canaugh had to say. Thorpe finally said, "I'll sum it up for the owners. I'll tell them that you think something could be going on, but it's too soon for you to tell. Okay?" Canaugh agreed. He asked if he should keep going to Montalvo's games and Thorpe told him, "I'll get back to you on that."

CHAPTER 19

July 1994

Canaugh was on his balcony reading the sports pages when his phone rang. Thorpe's intern was on the line and asked if Canaugh could make a meeting with Mr. Thorpe and the Crenshaws at 1:30. He said he could and was told to be there. Thorpe and the Crenshaws? said Canaugh to himself. It must be important. He went back to reading the box scores in the paper but couldn't concentrate. He was puzzled as to why he was being asked to attend a meeting with the Crenshaws. He'd had only one meeting with the Crenshaws and that was when he was hired. Maybe I'm getting fired today, he thought. He thought it possible but unlikely. He found it hard to relax. He decided that a walk over to Summit Avenue and then a walk along the Avenue was a good use of his time. It was a warm summer morning. There were lots of joggers and young moms with strollers out on Summit Avenue. Canaugh wished it was time for the meeting, and that he wouldn't have to wait. It was like waking up on the morning of a game when he was scheduled to pitch. The best way to deal with butterflies was always just to get started.

When Canaugh arrived at the Twins' offices and entered the meeting room, Thorpe and both Crenshaws were present, all three wearing anguished faces. Canaugh, unsure of what was coming next, dispensed with shaking hands and only nodded and said hello to the three of them in turn. Thorpe produced a plastic sleeve containing a one-page document. He passed it to Canaugh to read. It was a typed letter on plain white copy paper, without letterhead or date. It was unsigned. The letter stated that Isla Montalvo and Diego Montalvo, Frankie Montalvo's wife and son, were being held for ransom by members of a group called Los Perdido. Safe passage to the United States for the two of them could be made if Los Perdido were paid one and a half million dollars, with instructions to come later if Frankie and the Twins agreed. There was a phone number with more digits than usual. Canaugh looked up from the letter to see the three men staring at him, expecting him to speak. From his years as a cop and private investigator, he only had questions.

"How did this arrive?"

Thorpe produced another plastic sleeve containing a plain envelope on which was typed "Ian Thorpe, Personal and Confidential." Thorpe spoke. "It was dropped off late yesterday by Edina Couriers, a courier service."

Canaugh got only the words "What does the Courier service..." out before Thorpe said, "We contacted them. It was dropped off at their offices by someone who paid cash, but no one recalls the person. They don't have a security camera in that area."

"What does Montalvo know?" was Canaugh's next question.

Thorpe responded, "I talked to him, along with the manager in the manager's office last night. He wasn't scheduled to pitch. He claimed not to know anything about it, other than his wife and son are living in his hometown in Puerto Rico. As to when he found out about his wife being held or whether he was being extorted to throw meatballs when directed, he denied everything. As you might expect, he's very worried. Oh, and he doesn't have a million and a half dollars. He's under contract for not much above the minimum."

"What do you know about the phone number? Has anyone checked that out?"

Thorpe was emphatic in his response. "Well, we haven't called it, that's for sure. We checked with the phone company, and they say that it's a number in the Cayman Islands, but they can't tell us anything about whose number it is or more specifically where it might be located."

"Have you called the FBI, or the police either here or in Puerto Rico?"

Thorpe responded, "No. We want your input on that. We have doubts, such as does the FBI even have jurisdiction in Puerto Rico. Would we want to send in some trigger-happy Puerto Rican cops with guns blazing? We think not." Thorpe continued, "But our same thoughts apply when we met earlier. Once we involve cops of any kind, we lose control of the situation. Lose confidentiality. The media will be all over the story. National media. Those annoying videocam guys following me and Art home. We don't want that. Jesus," he finished with disdain.

"What do we know about the Los Perdido?"

Thorpe had an answer. "That's for you to find out. My hunch is that it's not some political or revolutionary group. More likely a front for a drug gang. Drug gangs are taking over all of South America and the Caribbean. The governments don't try to stop them. Kidnapping is one of the ways they make money. It's on the news. You likely won't find out anything. But try."

Art Crenshaw finally leaned forward and spoke quietly, as if he might be overheard outside the room. "We want a new stadium. We don't want, can't have in fact, any negative publicity about the Twins at this time. Dave, our PR guy, says that we can't have the public hear anything negative about us. Anything. So, we have to respond with care." Leon nodded in agreement.

There was a long silence while the three men looked at

Canaugh. Realizing that they were expecting him to provide a solution, he said, "Guys, I don't encounter this every day, so don't expect me to pull a rabbit out of a hat here. All I know is that in every situation I've been in, the most important thing you can ever do is to first get the facts." He stated the next four words slowly for emphasis. "Nail down the facts. We have to start by finding out if this letter is a genuine threat. The only way I can think of to do that at this moment is to call the number in the letter."

Thorpe spoke up, "I've thought about that. In the Mafia movies, the kidnappers prove they've got the hostage by cutting off an ear or a finger and sending it along in a package. I don't particularly want to be part of that."

"It's a risk, sure," said Canaugh. "But there's always a difference between Hollywood and real life. What if you have Montalvo listening in and asking a couple of questions to verify the situation. He's the only one that can identify his wife's voice."

Thorpe responded, "I can make that call with Frankie. If the number is in the Cayman's we'll probably have to arrange another call, assuming Frankie's wife is still in Puerto Rico. How about if you go down there first to see what you can see? Can you go tomorrow?"

Canaugh agreed that he could go. Thorpe said that he could have the Twins' traveling secretary make the necessary arrangements. He asked Canaugh to come back by 4:00 to pick up his plane ticket. Canaugh asked Thorpe for a copy of the letter.

"No. This is so sensitive, so explosive, that I don't want any copies made. I'm going to keep it in my office safe. Hope that's OK. We can't take any chances."

Canaugh shrugged and said, "Fine." He was mentally making a list of what he'd need to take with him to Puerto Rico. He considered taking a gun, his reliable friend when he got in a tight spot. It would be a hassle to get it onto two airplane flights, so perhaps it was best to buy one when he got to Puerto Rico. From what he'd heard over the years about Puerto Rico, it shouldn't be too hard.

When he got back to his apartment, Canaugh had only a couple of hours before he needed to go back to the stadium. How was he going to check out anything about Los Perdido in that period of time? He called Ike's courthouse number. His law clerk answered and told Canaugh, "Judge Brennan is on the bench now. I will have him call you when court ends." Canaugh snorted at her choice of words. "On the bench" in baseball was a bad thing. It meant that someone wasn't playing, usually because they weren't good enough or they were in the manager's doghouse. "On the bench" in the law was a good thing. It meant that court was in session and a judge was taking charge of the courtroom, giving someone their day in court. Ike called back in twenty minutes. Ike, as usual, started with his customary question.

"Canaugh, what do you know for sure?"

Canaugh was ready. "Everyone says I'm apathetic, but I don't care." He got a laugh from Ike.

"What's up?" Ike asked. "I don't fix parking tickets if that's your question. Just pay up, you putz."

Canaugh responded, "Since when did Irish guys start speaking Yiddish. Hey, I need to find out something about a group called Los Perdido. Do you have a law clerk or two that wants to take a break from deciding your cases to do a bit of research? I'm a little pressed for time, and I know you guys have resources that the common man doesn't have, particularly when it comes to the criminal element."

Canaugh could tell that Ike was curious. Ike responded, "To be clear, this office is not a public service for the citizens of St. Paul, even though Ramsey County spends its money on hockey rinks instead of libraries. You probably have no idea, but

I'm curious as to why you want to know."

"I can't explain due to the confidentiality agreement I signed. Due to your advancing years, you may not remember the contract I asked you to review a month or so ago."

"Helping the goddamn Twins. What do I get out of the deal?"

"You'll get what you're currently getting paid by the State of Minnesota."

Ike laughed. "Heck, I should get a lot more than that." His tone changed. "When do you need this by?"

Canaugh responded, "5:30 or 6:00, is that possible?"

The Judge whistled and said, "Don't you understand that this is a government operation? We quit at 4:30 here. Always have and always will. If me or my clerks are still in the courthouse after 4:30 there's a risk that we could get locked in. Why, I need to be careful leaving at 4:30 each day for fear of getting trampled on my way to the exits. I let you know what we come up with at quittin' time. Sorry, Vinny, that's all I can do for you today."

Canaugh was back in his apartment by 4:30, after hustling back from the Twins' offices. Ike called and said, "It's a dry hole, partner. We found nothing. Is that a surprise?"

Canaugh said, "Not really. Thanks a lot Ike. I appreciate it."

Ike asked, "Want to go fishing on the St. Croix tomorrow, late afternoon?"

"Sorry, can't. Going out of town. Can't say where."

Ike responded by singing in a hoarse off-key voice the chorus from Johnny Rivers' "Secret Agent Man".

Canaugh cut him off. "What an old-timer. Sometimes you're really embarrassing."

CHAPTER 20

July 1994

Canaugh was going to Puerto Rico. He didn't have that much experience making travel arrangements and was grateful that the Twins' traveling secretary told him he'd take care of it. Canaugh had picked up a printed itinerary and a set of tickets on Braniff Airlines. He would fly to Miami, and then pick up a connecting flight into San Juan. A rental car had been arranged for him. Thorpe had given him Frankie Montalvo's home address in Santa Isabel. Canaugh could see from the rental car company road map included in his itinerary envelope that Santa Isabel was on the south side of the island, about 60 miles from the airport in San Juan.

In Miami, he never left the air-conditioned airport, but he could see the condensation on the outside of the windows which told him that July in Miami was hot and humid. In San Juan, he had to walk across an asphalt parking lot to get to his rental car. He'd experienced heat and humidity playing minor league ball in small southern towns, but nothing like a summer afternoon in San Juan. He got lost a couple of times finding the highway that would take him south to Santa Isabela. It was Canaugh's first visit to Puerto Rico. Actually, it was his first visit anywhere outside the U.S. He'd played baseball with many Puerto Ricans, who said they loved the place but were glad to be in the U.S. Many baseball players referred to the place as "Porty Rico."

In the first half hour of his trip, Canaugh decided that Puerto Rico, an American possession, was a little bit American, but mostly Caribbean. Near the airport, he could see that most of the houses had iron bars over their windows for security. Some of the high-rise apartments had iron bars on windows up on the second and third floors, which Canaugh found a bit threatening. Once out of San Juan, he thought that the small towns seemed dirty and scruffy. There were lots of poor towns in the U.S., which he'd seen on his minor league bus rides, but they tended to be cleaner and in better repair than the island towns. He found the highway and the sights he was seeing to be somehow foreign to his experience, and he now understood the deep drive of the Puerto Rican ballplayers to get out of there.

There was an American presence, but not in a good way. He saw refineries and chemical plants with American names on their smokestacks like Dow and Exxon. Canaugh guessed that the American companies operated plants in Puerto Rico that they couldn't operate in the U.S due to the American pollution laws. Not far out of San Juan, the English words disappeared from road signs and billboards. The tropical trees and plants seemed to get closer to the road. He was finding it hard to relax on this trip.

Canaugh was uncertain about the need to go to Puerto Rico. When he'd asked Thorpe if he should go down to Montalvo's hometown, Thorpe seemed enthused. "Yes, go and see what you can see. We should be thorough." Canaugh didn't really have a plan, figuring that he would rely on his instincts once he got to Santa Isabel and would try to "see what he could see." Santa Isabel was not big, about 20,000 people. It was a coastal town with nice beaches, but it was too far from the San Juan airport and too small to draw many American tourists. The Twins' traveling secretary had made a reservation for him at the Las Brisas Hotel. Canaugh hoped that with a name of "The Breezes" that it would have the promise of cooler temperatures.

Canaugh had read that Santa Isabel was known in Puerto Rico as "The Land of Champions" because of the local emphasis on sports and the fact that many of its athletes had made it to the U.S. to play professional sports.

Canaugh checked into Las Brisas. It was a two-story whitewashed cement block building. The cement blocks had undoubtedly, over the years, helped the hotel endure the occasional hurricane that hit the island's south shore. Though neither fancy or new, it met the criteria of "cheap and cheerful". The desk clerk named Maria was warm and welcoming and she spoke excellent English, which Canaugh appreciated. He asked her a lot of questions about the town, careful not to give any indication of what his mission was other than to indicate that he was on vacation and that he might try some fishing. In a small town, Canaugh figured that news could travel fast.

Canaugh changed into shorts, a t-shirt, and a straw fedora. His wardrobe choice was partly to blend in as a tourist as much as possible, but mostly to deal with the heat and humidity of the late afternoon. Wearing flip-flops, he strolled on the sand, and on the sidewalk where there was one. He'd memorized the address for Montalvo's home. It was along the beach highway. Within ten minutes, Canaugh found the address. He stole glances at the house as he walked past it across the road, and then turned to head back to the hotel.

The house was nicer than most in the town, not unexpected because Canaugh figured that playing professional baseball in the U.S. would put a local guy at the top of the income ladder in this quiet beach town. There were no American companies visible in Santa Isabel, and it was uncertain how anyone made a living in the place. It was a two-story house with a large second floor balcony facing the ocean. The house had the typical colonial style, white with dark wood windows and doors. The roof had dark red steel panels with no overhang that could catch hurricane winds and rip the roof off. The house's current state was likely not original construction, but rather it was modified to deal with the storms, or perhaps even repaired because of one. As Canaugh made his way back to his hotel a tropical downpour started. He started to jog but the rain ended in minutes. He was drenched as he entered the lobby. "Got caught in a shower," he offered as an explanation for his appearance to Maria.

She said sympathetically, with a small hint of disdain for his mainlander's ignorance, "It rains here every day at four o'clock, but it only lasts a few minutes. See, the sun is out again." Canaugh made arrangements with her to borrow a beach chair for the next day.

The next day, Canaugh carried his folding canvas beach chair, and then with a bit of theatrics in case anyone was watching him, picked out a place to unfold the beach chair for maximum sun. He didn't really want any sun, so he was happy to find that the chair had a small canvas roof to cover his head. Years of playing baseball had caused all kinds of mysterious growths to appear on his fair Irish skin, which compelled him to visit a Highland Park dermatologist on a regular basis. He set his chair parallel to the ocean, as if to maximize his exposure to the rising sun. Facing east, he could see the beach walkers and the surf, but also keep an eye on the Montalvo residence without being obvious. He covered his exposed skin with sunblock and settled in with a newspaper, which he held at a height that allowed him to see his surroundings over the top of the pages. Of all the stakeouts he'd been on in his life, this was clearly the most enjoyable. He realized that he was getting paid well to sit on a tropical beach, and he thought of his father who'd spent hot sunny days on roofs pounding nails into shingles, trying not to fall off the roof.

After an hour there was no sign of life at Montalvo's house. He had no picture of Montalvo's wife, just opinion overheard in the Twins office that she was a beauty. Montalvo had a son, still small. By the second hour, Canaugh did see a man stroll out onto the balcony. He had on a print shirt and sunglasses. He stared at the waves for a few minutes while he smoked a cigarette. Canaugh noted the time on his watch. Soon the man disappeared back into the house. The significance of the man's appearance was unknown to Canaugh, though he pondered all sorts of possibilities.

Nothing else was visible at the house for the next half an hour. Canaugh realized that he was hungry, thirsty, and needed to use a bathroom. He left his chair and newspaper on the beach and walked a bit to a bodega he'd seen on his walk yesterday. He bought a beach towel, a sandwich, and two bottles of water and used the toilet. He asked for a paper bag to carry his purchases. Carrying the bag he strolled past the house, not on the beach side but instead on the sidewalk in front of the house. The house had a masonry arch over the front steps, with a black iron grill for a gate. He double-checked the house number for accuracy, and though he looked for a name plate on the mailbox or the gate, he couldn't find any.

Canaugh spent a couple more hours on the beach. The hot afternoon sun mostly emptied out the beach. Canaugh shifted his chair to face west. He spread the towel over his legs to avoid a sunburn. As he surveyed his pinkish arms, he made a mental note to buy and wear a long-sleeved t-shirt the next day. He kept glancing at the house, but he saw no sign of life. A little before 4:00 he rose, folded up his beach chair, and made it back to Las Brisas before the daily shower hit. As he took a shower, he wondered about the meaning of the day's surveillance. Did no activity at all have any meaning? Who was the man in Montalvo's house and why was he there?

Canaugh spent the second day on the beach just like the day before. He wore a long-sleeve t-shirt, and he had his towel to keep his legs covered. Nothing much happened at the house, except that the man appeared on the balcony twice to smoke a cigarette. He didn't see Montalvo's wife. He saw no other sign of life. When he got back to the hotel, he phoned Thorpe. He explained everything he saw (mostly what he didn't see) and told Thorpe that his instinct was a third day would not change anything. Canaugh didn't add that he was sunburned and bored and while a beach vacation in the winter appeals to all Minnesotans, a beach vacation in the heat of July wasn't that pleasant. Thorpe sighed when Canaugh finished his report. "OK, then," he said. "C'mon home. No need for a written report." Canaugh checked out of the hotel the next morning. In response to Maria's question about how he found his two days in Santa Isabel, he said, "Very relaxing." In response to her suggestion that he come back again, he only nodded and smiled. He drove back to San Juan. As he took his two flights home, his only thought was how glad he was to be leaving Puerto Rico behind.

CHAPTER 21

July 1994

Thorpe had convened another meeting with Canaugh and the Crenshaws in the Metrodome conference room that Canaugh had started to think of as the "Executive Cave". Thorpe took over the meeting from the start by saying, "Let's review where we are." He summarized Canaugh's trip to Puerto Rico as inconclusive. He summarized Canaugh's observations about watching Montalvo pitch both at the Metrodome and in Chicago and talked about the mystery of Signalman. He turned his attention to Canaugh as he summed up Canaugh's conclusions on the topic by saying, "Canaugh couldn't discern a pattern, but he thinks that something most likely is going on." As he was finishing his sentence, he started nodding vigorously at Canaugh. Canaugh didn't exactly agree with the words Thorpe had chosen to discuss Canaugh's thoughts, thinking that what Signalman was doing was still inconclusive, but he didn't choose to interrupt Thorpe or disagree with Thorpe's earnest nodding.

Thorpe continued, "I've given it a lot of thought and I think I have a solution to our problem. The club will give Montalvo a new contract. It will have a million and a half bonus, which will get paid to the outfit in the Cayman Islands. The new contract will be for three to five years. I'll have to work that out with his representative. He's a rising talent and deserves a new contract, a better contract anyway. He's definitely a keeper. The bonus money won't get paid until Montalvo's wife and boy are in the U.S. I'll have to work with our immigration lawyers to make that happen. We're signing so many foreign players these days that we're keeping those guys busy."

Thorpe paused. Canaugh had nothing to say. The Crenshaws just sat there blinking at first, but then they started nodding. Art finally spoke. "Yeah, makes sense. I like that Montalvo."

Thorpe didn't hesitate. "Well, that'll be our plan. We will keep the secrecy in place, except for the terms of the new contract which I have to report to the League, and I'll give my favorite columnist the scoop on the new contract when everything is done. I'll have you guys sign off as usual on the final contract terms once I've got something ready."

There was a pause while nothing was said. Finally, Thorpe said, "That's all I've got. Are we done?"

As the four men headed for the door, Thorpe grabbed Canaugh by the elbow and said in a quiet voice, "Canaugh, your job is done. Can you get to me your final billing and expense report by next Monday? I'll see that you get paid right way." As Thorpe walked Canaugh out to the lobby he offered his hand and as he shook Canaugh's hand he said, "Thank you for helping us out. I may have some more work for you next season, so let's stay in touch." He smiled and slapped Canaugh on the back as Canaugh departed.

Canaugh walked slowly to his car. *Big business*, he thought to himself. Canaugh had just witnessed the Crenshaws spend over five million dollars in a ten-minute meeting. Canaugh spent almost as much time in the supermarket doing the math as part of choosing what laundry detergent to buy.

About three weeks later Canaugh saw an item in Sid Truman's column in the Tribune about Montalvo getting a sizable new contract extension. The matter was now complete, Canaugh figured. His summer adventure was over.

CHAPTER 22

September 1994

Canaugh needed to see a doctor. He'd always been wary of doctors for a few reasons. His father had distrusted doctors. He would always advise Canaugh and all who would listen "Never go to the doctors' office. They'll just find something wrong with you." Eventually his father was proven right, though it took many years. In 1970 his father's stomach pain was so bad he ventured into the small clinic in Albany. After some preliminary tests and a referral to some specialists in St. Cloud, he was told that he had stomach cancer and that, given his age and the progress of his disease, there was nothing the doctors could do for him other than to advise him to get his affairs in order. He died a month later.

Canaugh's mother disliked doctors but her phobia was related to the cost involved. For most of their lives, until they became Medicare-eligible, the family didn't have health insurance. In his junior high days, in response to pressure from his friends and the coaches, Canaugh told his parents he wanted to go out for football and asked them to sign the waiver papers provided by the school. His mother wailed about the possibility of his getting hurt and how they couldn't afford for him to get any medical treatment. His father, as he did on many family issues, offered no opinion and simply deferred to his mother to make the decision. Canaugh didn't play football.

In his days playing professional baseball, Canaugh would occasionally have problems with his arm, or some muscle pain elsewhere in his body related to throwing a baseball with maximum force. He would be sent to team doctors, who would examine and test his arm. In the low minor leagues, the doctors seemed to have a bias towards favoring the owners over the players, and they tended to clear the players to return to the team with a minimum of treatment and days missed. He and the other pitchers discussed their experience seeing team doctors, and all expressed concern about whether they were getting good impartial medical advice. It was rare that a player had the resources or willingness to go to an independent doctor. "You gotta be your own doctor" was an expression Canaugh had heard many times among minor league players.

Canaugh had been experiencing some chest pain from time to time. He'd done some reading and found that the causes of chest pain in men exceeded a dozen in number, many of them minor and capable of simply going away over time. However, one of them was more serious than all the others, which could lead to a potential heart attack. Despite a lifetime of ignoring various aches and pains, a pain that had the potential to kill him got Canaugh's attention. He made an appointment at the Minneapolis Heart Institute in the scruffy neighborhood on Chicago Avenue between downtown Minneapolis and Lake Street. His mother's concern about the cost of visiting the doctor, never forgotten by Canaugh, could be ignored now that Canaugh had a problem he considered to be serious. He still had so-so health insurance he'd converted to a personal policy when he left the police force.

Canaugh found the clinic located on the second floor of the Abbott-Northwestern Hospital. The clinic was sizable. The dignified sign containing a small photo and an engraved brass nameplate for each cardiologist was at the doorway leading out of the spacious waiting room. The waiting room had upholstered chairs for over fifty patients mostly facing in random directions so that patients and visitors would not end up staring at each other. Canaugh, due to habits formed in many years of work as a policeman and a private investigator, took a chair in the corner of the room where he could get a good look at most everyone present, including those entering and leaving. Unsure of finding the clinic, he'd arrived early and, aware of the propensity of doctors to frequently be running behind schedule, settled in for a long wait. He'd brought along the morning paper.

He was surprised to see Signalman enter the room, very much the same as he appeared in the Metrodome. He was even wearing his usual red and blue Twins jacket and a Twins hat on top of his abundant white hair. Signalman, after checking in at the counter, took a seat not far from Canaugh. Canaugh was a bit startled to see Signalman in a clinic waiting room and considered many alternatives. Had Signalman tailed him here? Unlikely, decided Canaugh. He had a sixth sense about being tailed and had no indication that anyone had followed him over from St. Paul. Besides, a person tailing someone doesn't sit down right in the line of vision of the person they are following. After all, the cardinal principle of tailing a person is to not be seen. Canaugh wanted to keep his eye on Signalman. He pretended to read his newspaper. He rotated his gaze around the room, keeping Signalman in the corner of his eye.

Then Signalman touched his nose with his right hand! *What the bloody hell?* thought Canaugh. He looked around the room to see if Signalman was giving a sign to someone, but Canaugh couldn't see anyone paying attention to Signalman. Canaugh looked away toward the desk, keeping Signalman in his field of vision. He saw Signalman touch his nose again. Canaugh, without moving his head, looked around to see who might be paying attention to Signalman, but Canaugh couldn't detect anyone. A nurse appeared in the doorway and said the name "Thomas", following the new protocol that public announcements used only the first name of patients. Signalman rose and followed the nurse down the hall. Canaugh's mind raced as he considered various alternatives for what he had just witnessed.

A few minutes later, a nurse appeared and announced "Vincent" and Canaugh glanced around. Seeing no one stirring, he rose and followed the nurse. He was not used to having his full first name used, though the name "Vince" had been announced frequently during his pitching days.

Canaugh followed the nurse into the small exam room and answered her questions about his date of birth and his symptoms. While she put the blood pressure cuff on him and began squeezing the bulb, Canaugh said, in the most disinterested tone he could muster under the circumstances, "There was a guy out in the waiting room who kept touching his nose. Kinda odd."

The nurse's response was quite abrupt, and she said without looking at him, "I can't discuss the condition of any other patient."

To Canaugh, someone who wouldn't answer his questions was just a challenge to be overcome, like facing the best hitter in the batting order. He decided to act kind of clownish, and so he chuckled and said, "It was sure odd to see. I wonder what's troubling him."

The nurse looked kind of grim and said nothing for a while, and then finally said, "Something like that could be Tourette Syndrome." She made eye contact with Canaugh to let him know that she wasn't going to discuss the matter further, and then added, "It will be a few minutes before the doctor will be in to see you." Likely a fib, thought Canaugh as he picked up a magazine. He tore out a card offering an introductory subscription. He took out his pen, wrote "Tur-ette Syndrome" on the card, and tucked the card and pen back in his pocket, out of a habit of many, many years as a cop.

Eventually the doctor arrived, a pleasant young woman

with a name badge that said Dr. Lynn Robertson M.D. *It's a changing world,* thought Canaugh as she had him remove his shirt and listened intently to his heartbeat through her stethoscope. She told him that the clinic would run some tests and take a chest x-ray, and that he would need to spend the morning at the clinic. Canaugh waited patiently as a series of nurses and technicians did a blood draw and led him to a room where they did x-rays. Through the process, Canaugh forgot about the pain in his chest and his concern over that problem, and thought only about the nurse's words "Tourette Syndrome." A few more stops at a very casual pace for a urine test, an EKG, and a sliding ride through something that looked like an oversized beige donut, and he was sent to the waiting room again to wait. There was no sign of Signalman, though Canaugh had taken another chair where he could observe all patients coming or going. In half an hour, he was back in the room again with Doctor Robertson.

She questioned him about his diet. Canaugh thought he saw a faint flicker of her disapproval in his answer, particularly when he talked about eating hot dogs at the ballpark that summer. Finally, she said, "We don't think there is anything abnormal about your heart, based upon the test results. Our working diagnosis at this moment is heartburn from too much fat in your diet. No more hot dogs, please. Buy some antacids at your drugstore and take them when you feel symptoms again. I'm going to make a referral to our Cardio Education program, which covers diet and exercise for a heart-healthy lifestyle. I recommend that you follow the advice given. If you have any more trouble, please come back and see us as soon as possible." Canaugh had mostly stopped listening to everything she said after the word "heartburn" because he realized that it was nothing serious. He had dodged the bullet he feared. The nurse came in and gave him some documents which he tucked into his jacket pocket without reading, vowing vaguely to himself to read them someday.

After leaving the heart clinic, he made his way to the main entrance of the hospital and found the Information Desk. At the desk, he learned where the medical library was and that it was open to patients. He found the library in an out-of-the-way place on the fourth floor and got some help from the librarian. He sat down with a medical encyclopedia and found the pages on Tourette Syndrome. Within a few minutes he learned that Tourette's Syndrome involved involuntary repetitive motions, usually appearing during adult years, and while there were some therapies that diminished its effects, there was no cure. According to what Canaugh read, nose or face-touching was a common behavior, though on the spectrum of all possible Tourette behaviors, it was rather mild. Some cases of Tourette's involved involuntary verbal outbursts or head-snapping.

Canaugh experienced a cold feeling deep in his stomach. Signalman hadn't been signaling to Montalvo. Canaugh had jumped to the wrong conclusion, and it was a big error on his part. It was the difference-maker in his conclusion. What did it mean if Signalman was not part of any plot? Canaugh had an instinct to get home, back to his apartment to think things over. He drove back to St. Paul on the I-94 freeway, but took the early exit at Cretin Avenue, realizing that he was lost in thought and a busy freeway was not a safe place for him to be driving. He took Cretin down to Grand, turned and headed back home on the well-shaded back streets of St. Paul. Back in his apartment, he paid no attention to the fact that he'd received the coveted "it's nothing" type of diagnosis and had something to celebrate. Instead, he recalled all the events of the summer, examining them as if they were evidence.

He started at the beginning, the very first meeting. Recalling Thorpe's words "You've been specially chosen" gave him chills as he recalled it, considering that Thorpe could have meant something else entirely. He recalled the Confidentiality Agreement, the only one he'd ever signed which was unnecessary except to protect Thorpe. He remembered

Thorpe's instruction to discuss the matter only with Thorpe. He recalled that Thorpe had the only copy of the ransom note and he didn't permit any copies to be made. Canaugh realized with a bit of panic that he'd made some errors in assessing Signalman. He didn't stay to watch Signalman after Montalvo was done pitching. He only went to Montalvo's games. Of course, Signalman wouldn't have been at the game in Chicago. He was a Twins season ticket holder. Despite his years of experience, Canaugh had attached significance to what was just a coincidence.

It hit him that Thorpe worked for two members of the Crenshaw family. One was a wealthy owner who seemed mostly detached. Art Crenshaw appeared to have his eye on the pleasures of retiring and enjoying his large fortune. The other, his son, had solid academic credentials but was naïve about the dark side of corporate business in general, and not that knowledgeable about professional baseball. The Crenshaws, Canaugh was realizing, were vulnerable to someone determined to take advantage of them.

Canaugh thought of Montalvo's new contract, granted mid-season, which was a bit out of the ordinary. Players having good seasons did get locked up for future years, though it was rare to do it mid-season. Most contract negotiation took place in the off-season, when players and management weren't distracted. Canaugh thought that the structure of the contract was a bit out of the ordinary, too, with a large signing bonus compared to the total contract value. Thorpe had said that the bonus money had been wired to a bank in the Cayman Islands. Canaugh wondered how a new contract with a bonus going elsewhere got the approval of Montalvo's agent. Bonus money frequently got paid to players' agents. As time went on and agents became a bigger part of professional baseball, the agents took on the role of money managers, too. Like musicians and actors who'd made it to the big time, agents now provided ballplayers more than just representation in negotiations with owners. They invested money for players and paid their bills. It made sense for some players, thought Canaugh. Many of the players who made it to the majors weren't born in America. Many of the American-born players had only a high school education. Canaugh had concluded long ago that he and Judy could manage the hundreds of dollars a month he made playing minor league baseball, but managing hundreds of thousands of dollars, if he ever got to major league status, would require some professional help.

He decided that he needed to find out who Montalvo's agent was. But how to do it? Canaugh's instincts told him that there was some risk in asking Thorpe, and that there was even some risk in Thorpe finding out that Canaugh was asking that question.

Canaugh knew that the most knowledgeable sports reporter in the Twin Cities was Wally Charles. Canaugh had read his columns in the St. Paul Pioneer Press for twenty years. He'd met him once or twice both in his days as a police lieutenant and as private security for the Harrington banking family interests. He doubted that Charles would remember him, though it was possible. Mostly he knew of the man's habits. Wally Charles covered baseball games from the press box in the Metrodome. He would have half his game story written by the fifth inning. After watching hundreds of Twins games, Wally had a knack for knowing what was going to happen in terms of the final outcome. Wally had developed certain understandings. The first team to ten hits was overwhelmingly likely to win that night. He knew who the Twins would bring in to pitch in relief on any given night, because he kept track of who'd been used the night before and what the manager would do on any occasion. He knew which pitchers and batters were on a good streak or were slumping. He was something of a legend for his habit of saying "That's the ballgame" in the press box at a critical moment of a hit, an error, or an out, and he was right almost all the time.

Wally had done his homework by hanging out near

the players before the game, trading on personal relationships developed during the Twins' spring training (first Orlando, then Ft. Myers) both at the ballpark and at the team hotel. His bosses at the paper knew that he was a boost for circulation, and while they didn't pay him (or any other reporter for that matter) generously, they increased his expense account annually so that he could buy drinks and meals for players and the coaching staff while he chatted them up for useful information. Due to rumors Canaugh had heard in the organization, Wally liked to file his story within half an hour after the game was over with, and then repair to his favorite watering hole where he could enjoy cocktails and swapping baseball stories with a regular gang of guys who would seek him out. Whether they sought him out because they enjoyed his company or because they enjoyed having him pick up the tab, abusing his employer's expense account in the process, was never made clear.

Canaugh made his way that evening to Al's, a bar on Excelsior Avenue just outside the Minneapolis city limits that had a plain interior. Due mostly to its suburban location, it was a notch or two above the basic Minnesota dive bar. He breathed a sigh of relief to see Wally in a large corner booth with a few others, though there was room for one more. Canaugh ordered a draft Coors and wandered over to the booth. He asked Wally politely if he could join them, observing the social grace of paying tribute to the host of the gathering. He got waved into the huddle. He introduced himself to Wally and the others as a retired police detective. He was hopeful that his former job would earn him some immediate respect, and that he would likely be viewed as having good stories with possibly some inside information on the city's politicians and criminals. People who hung out in bars believed that there was occasionally some overlap between the two.

Canaugh told Wally that they had met before. Being reasonably certain that Wally was under the influence of a couple of drinks by this point, Canaugh embellished some stories of how often they'd met and what the circumstances were. Canaugh bought a round and slowly sipped his beer while the others drank up with gusto. After an hour or so trading baseball stories with Wally and the others, Canaugh felt that he was in the embrace of the group. Canaugh waited for the right moment to introduce the new topic of Montalvo's contract. Canaugh waited patiently as Wally offered his opinion, and when Wally got to the point of saying that the Twins had overpaid Montalvo, Canaugh pounced. "He must have a good agent," Canaugh said. "Who's representing him?"

Wally had the answer. "Here's the weird part. He used to be represented by Tommy Tucker, one of the best. But Montalvo dismissed him in spring training. He doesn't have one. He appears to have taken advantage of the Twins all by himself."

Maybe not, thought Canaugh to himself realizing that he couldn't say anything. With his question answered, he picked the most graceful time possible to depart from Wally's booth. He smiled and slapped a couple of backs on his way out and headed to the parking lot. Everything was now clicking into place as to what Thorpe had done. Canaugh drove very slowly on the way home, lost in thought. It was now clear to him that he'd been used by Thorpe just to provide authentic cover for Thorpe's plan to fleece the Crenshaws. He didn't feel good about that.

CHAPTER 23

September 1994

It was 9:00 on a Sunday morning. Canaugh and Ike were at Durgin's Marina in Forest Lake renting a fishing boat. Forest Lake is a town on a big lake, also named Forest Lake, about 30 miles north of St. Paul. Canaugh and Ike had gone fishing on Forest Lake dozens of times, and they always rented a 16-foot Lund aluminum fishing boat at Durgin's Marina. There are thousands of 16-foot aluminum fishing boats with 60-horse motors owned by Minnesota fishermen. Canaugh had decided that if the Minnesota Legislature ever got around to naming a State Boat (to go along with the State Muffin, State Insect, and State Soup) it would be the 16-foot aluminum Lund boat.

There was a slight haze on the lake that morning, which, until the sun burned it off, gave a golden cast to the water and sky. The water was calm, only the classic "walleye chop" found on Minnesota lakes on great days for fishing. As usual, Canaugh took the helm of the motor and steered the boat out into the lake. There were a few fishing boats close to the shore, but Canaugh headed out towards the center of the 35 square-mile lake. Ike sat in the front of the boat. The noise of the 60-horse Evinrude prevented much conversation. Once the boat was a few miles from shore, Ike turned to Canaugh and said, "Jesus, Canaugh, there won't be any fish out here. It's too deep."

"I'm coming out here to talk, not fish," Canaugh responded.

"That's a relief," said Ike. "I thought I was being kidnapped."

Once they were miles from shore, Canaugh cut the motor and let the boat drift in the slight morning breeze. He explained, "I am going to breach my Confidentiality Agreement, the one you looked at, and I wanted some privacy."

"It's not like we needed to travel into International Waters to do so," said Ike. He looked around at the distant shore and tops of the buildings in the town. "Though in a couple more goddamn miles I think we'd be there."

"This is a good time to pour yourself a cup of coffee," said Canaugh, nodding at the Thermos bottle. "This is going to take a little time."

Ike poured himself some coffee into the cup-like lid of the Thermos and said, "What ya got?"

Canaugh told Ike all about his work for the Twins, including his first meeting with Thorpe and the Crenshaws, and how he'd sized everyone up. He explained how he'd sat in his Metrodome seat charting each pitch made by Frankie Montalvo, and how he'd spend the days in between at his dining table analyzing his notes, looking for a pattern. He told about the letter Thorpe had received and Canaugh's trip to Puerto Rico. He told Ike about the fan in the front row touching his nose, and how Canaugh had started charting nose-touching. It sounded crazy in the telling. He told about Frankie getting a new contract, with the signing bonus getting wired to the Cayman Islands, because Frankie had dismissed his agent. He got to the part about later encountering Signalman at the clinic and his subsequent epiphany about what had really happened. He wrapped up his story with his conclusions about what Thorpe had really done with Frankie's contract, and that Thorpe had ended up with the bonus money.

Ike had listened patiently, sipping his coffee, taking off his windbreaker at one point because the early fall morning was warming up. When Canaugh finished, Ike said nothing for a long time. Finally, he stood and took a leak over the side of the boat. "I'm taking advantage of being so far offshore no one can see me."

Ike could see from Canaugh's face that Canaugh wanted some direction from him about what to do next. Ike finally spoke. "What a great story. Your problem is that you have no proof. Decisions should ideally be made on the basis of evidence. You have no evidence. You have only a circumstantial case, built upon your suspicions as to what happened. No prosecutor would touch it based on what you've got. All you've got is a charming story. It's plausible all right, but there's not much you can do with it, absent coming up with some proof. I take it that you've thought about how you can find some evidence and haven't come up with anything." He then was silent for a long time, until he continued.

"This sounds like a perfect crime to me. You've got only one guy in on it, maybe two counting Frankie, but his role is minor and he's just a young immigrant, undoubtedly kept in the dark to a great extent by Thorpe. Normally you'd follow the money, but in this case the money disappeared into the black hole of the Cayman bank secrecy laws. They have no treaties with the U.S. My brothers and sisters on the federal bench have told me about the frustration in getting information they need for the financial fraud cases that come before them. It's a closed and bolted door."

"The Crenshaws undoubtedly trust Thorpe, and it appears that they don't have suspicions or tight control over the guy. Trust." Ike snorted and paused a bit. "One of the things that amazed me after I'd been on the bench for a few years is how often misplaced trust is a factor in cases that come to court. The world couldn't operate without some trust, if you think about it, but trust can be undeserved. You see it in divorce cases, criminal cases, business fraud cases, all kinds of cases. There are plenty of people who aren't trustworthy, but nobody walks around with that label on their forehead. The surest clue that I've found over the years is that people that aren't trustworthy don't trust anyone else. Perhaps some psychologists can figure that out some day, but I can't explain it. But enough of me philosophizing. How can I help you, Canaugh?"

"I don't want him to get away with it. It bothers me. What can I do?"

Ike turned and faced Canaugh so that he was sure he had Canaugh's complete attention. "Look closely at how this guy operates. Let's assume that Thorpe planned this whole thing, just as you say. His planning had to include everything you could think of if you figured out what he was up to. He's probably worked on this for a couple years. You've had only a month. Whatever you've thought of, he's ready for it."

"You want me to give up? To let him get away with it?" Canaugh shook his head. "That's not right."

Ike snorted. "Who are you? The Lone Ranger? Let's say you go to someone with the story you just told me. The cops, the Crenshaws, the papers, you name it. They will ask you for your proof, of which you have none. Then the cat will be out of the bag, and you will find out what Thorpe has planned for you. If you're lucky, you'll only be discredited or ridiculed. Perhaps framed for something you didn't do. For sure you'll be sued by the Twins lawyers for violating the Confidentiality Agreement, which for sure you'll lose, and then you'll be broke. Worst case, you'll end up on the slab. Perhaps a fall down a long flight of stairs. A fall from an open window. Or the most common one that happens to important witnesses. You'll return home and 'surprise' a 'burglar' in the act, who happens to be packing a gun. There's a lot of money at stake. One of my maxims I learned from delivering papers in my small town growing up. 'Stay away from the big mean dogs.'"

"Killed. You think I could get killed?"

"Is there a lot of money at stake? Is this a powerful guy? Hell, ya. Thorpe's got a nice job, good pay, status in the community, trophy wife, the red carpet wherever he goes. He'll want to keep all that. Be careful, Canaugh. Don't let him find out that you've figured out what he did. I don't want anything to happen to you."

"Ike, I'm surprised to hear you say that."

"Well, I was just being polite. I'm Irish Catholic. The only emotions I'm capable of are guilt and despair. But kidding aside, promise me you won't do anything stupid." When Canaugh didn't respond, he repeated it. "Don't do anything stupid." There was silence for a while and Ike said, "I don't think I'm getting through to you. Look, I realize that there were a lot of things in your life that didn't go the way you wanted them to. Some sad stuff. Baseball, your wife. You deserved better. But don't get righteous. I see in my courtroom how much trouble the righteous can get into. There's usually a bad outcome. In this world, you've just got to get along." There was another long pause.

Canaugh finally said, "We'll see. Let's fish for an hour. We've got the boat rented for half a day, after all."

Ike sighed. "OK, but what say for a change we go where the fish might possibly be."

CHAPTER 24

September 1994

"Don't do anything stupid" was the advice that Ike had given to Canaugh. Canaugh pondered it as he paced around his apartment after the morning spent fishing with Ike. Canaugh didn't even turn on the lights as the afternoon turned to dusk. "Don't do anything stupid" was a cliché and was likely the most useless advice anyone could give. Parents commonly used that expression with teens. Canaugh recalled from his teen years hearing advice like that both at his house and in the houses of his high school friends. For one thing, it was rarely obvious to the listener what qualified as "stupid". For teen boys, hardly anything seems stupid, and as for those few things that were recognizable by them as stupid, an admonishment not to do them often served more as a challenge than an effective prohibition.

What was "stupid" in Canaugh's dilemma? Surely Ike meant making charges against Thorpe that wouldn't stick, resulting in Canaugh's losing his assets, his reputation, and possibly his life. Canaugh was considering all options. He did have an option of saying nothing, but that would bother him as time went by. Canaugh knew himself well enough to know that having Thorpe get away with his elaborate fraud was bothering him greatly only a few days after discovery. Canaugh was sure it would only aggravate him even more over time. He considered that option "stupid" also.

As dusk turned to dark, Canaugh opened a can of Old Milwaukee and sipped it, sitting in the dark, while he pondered other possible options. He could go to the Crenshaws, father and son, but he had no proof, just a theory, a bundle of "what if's". Ike was right, he wouldn't be taken seriously. Canaugh realized that other options included his making the effort to find evidence that would prove what Thorpe had done. He could go to the cops, local or federal, but he had the same problem. No proof, and there was a high risk that Thorpe would be made aware that Canaugh had flapped his lips to the cops. Thorpe likely had friends in the hierarchy of the law enforcement agencies. In his years at the MPD, he'd heard stories about how the people at the top of the chain of command got free box seat tickets to the games.

He could go to the newspaper writers. He considered that only briefly, until he realized that the newspapers were beholden to the Twins. The Twins gave them plenty of copy for their readers and could grant or withhold access to the players and coaches, all of whom were the Twins employees. Besides, newspapers didn't have investigative reporters anymore. They wanted their stories gift wrapped and handed to them.

He could go to the television reporters, but the TV people competed with the print reporters for the Twins' favor. They also could lose access to the Twins if they did anything unfriendly. Canaugh scoffed at his own notion that the TV stations might be interested in what he had to say. The TV stations in Minneapolis only reported on things after they happened. They didn't have real reporters, just people who looked good on TV and coveted access to players and the front office. It was 1994. TV provided entertainment, not news. Contact Major League Baseball? Based on everything he'd read, Canaugh agreed with Thorpe's assessment regarding a lack of talent and energy in that organization. Besides, Thorpe was an insider in that particular club of rich and powerful men and Canaugh was just an outsider, utterly without status.

Perhaps he could find a way to defraud Thorpe out of the money, as a way to give Thorpe a just outcome. Canaugh dismissed the thought as soon as he thought of it. Canaugh considered himself smart, but not smarter or more sophisticated than a man like Thorpe. Just to attempt fraud, Canaugh knew, was itself a crime, and he wasn't going to go that route, no matter how justified he felt. He thought of Judy, and how she wouldn't stand for him attempting something like that.

Canaugh had come to believe, based on his days as a police detective, that a criminal will always overlook at least one detail. He thought of the Mickey Rourke character's advice to the lawyer contemplating murder in Canaugh's favorite movie "Body Heat." Essentially the advice was that even if you're good, you can't think of everything when planning a major crime. "What didn't Thorpe think of?" The question occupied Canaugh past midnight until he fell asleep in his chair.

In the morning, after a shower and a cup of coffee, Canaugh took the bus to downtown St. Paul. He didn't know how long his errand would take and he didn't want to pay all-day downtown parking rates. His destination was the James J. Hill Reference Library. One of the most distinguished buildings in St. Paul, the ornate building looked out over Rice Park. Inside he looked for and found a librarian with a helpful face. She helped him find the books he wanted. He found a table and began his reading. He wasn't anywhere close to done by mid-day and he was hungry. He left his books at the desk and explained that he'd return after lunch. He felt frugal. *Watching my nickels and dimes must be the theme of the day*, he thought as he walked over to a nearby deli for a ham salad sandwich. He returned and spent until 4:00 in the library, at which point he re-shelved the books he'd been reading and caught the bus back to his apartment. Canaugh couldn't recall riding a bus since his days in the minor leagues. The buses in St. Paul were clean and nearly new, and Canaugh was pleasantly surprised that they had air conditioning. *My, the world has changed*, Canaugh thought as he got off at his stop on Grand Avenue and walked the few blocks back home, his mind churning with the information he'd found in the library.

The next day he went back to the library, only this time he brought along a tablet and some pens so that he could make some notes. Both were tucked into an inexpensive nylon briefcase with the Twins logo, which Thorpe had given him for his role as a scout. Canaugh had a new list of topics he wanted to read about that morning. The librarian noticed the Twins logo and seemed impressed with him, happy to be assisting the fit and friendly man with ice blue eyes. His list of requests didn't seem to fit any pattern and so she was puzzled about his mission, though she recognized that he seemed highly earnest in his research.

Canaugh read all morning, taking notes from time to time, until it was time for lunch. Canaugh knew about Original Coney Island, a dive bar in St. Paul that served good hot dogs, popular with cops and anyone seeking an inexpensive meal. He had good memories of previous visits to the place, some with Judy when they stopped in before a movie. He walked from the library all the way to St. Peter Street but when he got to the front door of the joint, he had second thoughts. The smell of stale beer and hot dogs cooking suddenly didn't appeal to him, and so he turned and walked back to the sandwich shop he'd found the day before. At age 64 he doubted that he had the stomach for digesting hot dogs without distress anymore. Canaugh again spent the afternoon in the library and then took the bus back to his neighborhood. It was a nice afternoon. He could see the first hints of fall in the yellowing leaves of the maple trees. To get some exercise, he took the long way home, stopping at a Greek restaurant on Grand Avenue to get a take-out dinner.

Canaugh woke up with more ideas the next morning and despite his being tired of the routine of spending the day in the library, he felt the need to give it one more day. The same librarian was behind the counter and gave him a friendly smile and greeting. "My name's Carol," she said, which was about an aggressive a flirtation as a Minnesota librarian could manage. Canaugh read past lunch time and didn't go out for lunch. When Canaugh turned his books back in at the main desk, Carol asked a bit hopefully, "Will we see you tomorrow?"

"Oh, I hope so," he replied, keeping it vague and not wanting to disappoint her. Canaugh walked all the way to Mickey's Diner, another favorite hangout for cops, and a theatrical relic of another age in downtown St. Paul. He ordered a hamburger, passed on the fries, and had a cup of coffee. The price was right. From the diner, he walked to Dayton's Department Store because he knew that the store had a travel agency. In the travel agency offices, he met with an available agent in her cubicle. He said that he wanted to purchase a ticket to Miami. When asked when he wanted to go, he inquired if it made any difference in price. "Oh no," he was told by the travel agent. "Fares are all regulated. The price is the same no matter what day you want to go."

"Then I'll go tomorrow," said Canaugh, calculating the things he needed to do to prepare for his trip. He picked a day three days later for his return flight.

"Do you want to pay for your trip with your Dayton's credit card?" he was asked.

Canaugh declined and said that he could be back in fifteen minutes to exchange cash for his ticket. When he returned to pick up his ticket, the agent asked him if he needed help making a hotel reservation or renting a car. He smiled, and then declined. "I can manage that by myself." Canaugh took the bus back home after leaving the department store. Packing was easy. He wouldn't need much for a short trip. He also realized that he didn't have much in the way of clothes.

CHAPTER 25

September 1994

Canaugh waited patiently in the lobby of the Woodhill Country Club in Wayzata. He'd been in most Twin City country clubs working as a police detective or private investigator. Woodhill, Minnesota's most-prestigious country club, had the same shabby-chic furnishings as most of the country clubs Canaugh had visited, except for the newest ones which had new paint, furniture, and drapes in their effort to impress. Canaugh had parked his car at the very end of the parking lot. He decided that a six-year-old Ford loaded with boxes would look out of place among the shiny new luxury cars parked near the clubhouse.

Canaugh had found, by calling Art Crenshaw's secretary, that Art and Leon Crenshaw would be playing golf Saturday morning at Woodhill. By calling the starter and pretending to be a member checking his tee time, he found out when the Crenshaws had started. He'd timed his arrival for four hours later so that he could hopefully intercept them after they finished their round and before they headed to the dining room or the bar. He had in his hand a large brown envelope containing an eleven-page letter he'd prepared. Canaugh had learned to type in his senior year in high school, though he wasn't an able student in that class. He mostly used the hour to flirt with the sophomore girls in class and goof around with other guys who were headed for college but considered typing to be women's work. Mostly he remembered his teacher's regular admonition "Canaugh, quit fooling around." Once he'd made detective grade with the Minneapolis Police, he was expected to type up reports for use by the County Attorney's office for prosecution of crimes, an aspect of police work that is overlooked in television shows about cops. He developed some accuracy, but not much speed. An eleven-page letter, double-spaced, took him two full days on the Selectric typewriter he'd rented from a store near Macalester College. On the envelope, he'd printed in block letters "Confidential" and "To be Opened by Addressee Only". It would have looked better if he'd used rubber stamps with those messages, like lawyers used, but he didn't want to search to buy them.

The receptionist at Woodhill was protective of the members' privacy and had curtly informed Canaugh that he could wait in the lobby, but could not have access to other parts of the Club property. She had promised to leave a message with the starter that Mr. Crenshaw had a guest waiting to see him in the lobby. After half an hour of waiting, Canaugh was frustrated, and began planning a ruse he could use to make his way to wait by the 18th hole. Just as he was about to stand up and do an end run outdoors around the Club's gatekeeper, the two Crenshaws appeared through the double doors that separated the lobby from the other facilities of the Club. They were dressed in their golf clothes, lots of plaid, including pastel-colored hats with the Club's name on them.

"Canaugh, this is a surprise," said Art Crenshaw. Canaugh was good at reading people, but he couldn't tell if Crenshaw was annoyed with him surprising Crenshaw at his country club. Crenshaw, successful in business, had learned how to keep a good poker face in any situation.

Canaugh extended the envelope. "Sorry to bother you on a

Saturday, but I'm on my way out of town. This is important, and I wanted to make sure that you got it." Art Crenshaw tentatively reached for the envelope and handed it off to his son. "Care to join us for lunch?" he asked heartily with obvious insincerity.

"Oh, thank you," Canaugh gushed, a bit phony, aware that having lunch in the members' dining room was an enormous favor being extended to a working-class snoop by a member of the privileged class. "But as I said, I'm on my way out of town and want to get going."

"If we have questions, can we call you?" Leon asked.

"Sure. You can ask Thorpe." Canaugh's face broke into a wry smile, aware of the double entendre joke he was about to make. "He has my number."

Canaugh returned to his car. He'd filled the gas tank the night before. It was nearly 1:00 and he'd hoped to get to Denver today but doubted that was possible and figured that he'd be spending the night someplace in Nebraska. He headed down Interstate 35 towards Des Moines. As he drove past Owatonna to the Iowa border, he mentally checked off all the steps he'd taken to implement his plan. He had prepared and delivered to the Crenshaws his accusation against Thorpe with all the information he had available to him, and suggestions for them on how to find out more. He'd given notice at his apartment and cut a deal with the management company to give them all of his furniture in exchange for his last month's rent. He'd packed all the things he decided that he would need in his new home. He hadn't told anyone about his plans because secrecy was important, and he hated to lie to his friends.

He left a forwarding address at the St. Paul Post Office to a small business mailbox and copy center in Eau Claire, Wisconsin, which in turn had been instructed to forward all mail to a Post Office box rented in the name of Addison Clark Company in Albuquerque. "Addison" and "Clark" were two streets in Chicago, and their intersection had been the site of

Wrigley Field since 1914. As far as Canaugh was concerned, Wrigley Field was one of the most sacred sites in all of baseball. Canaugh's destination wasn't Albuquerque but instead Santa Fe, one hour north of there on Interstate 25. None of the mail forwarding documentation in both places had Canaugh's name on it. He paid a year's rent in advance on each mailbox. He didn't expect much mail and he figured that he could journey into Albuquerque every now and then to check the mailbox. Once he rented a mailbox in Santa Fe, he could set up another anonymous forwarding address.

Canaugh had a name picked out for his new identity, which was Harvey Hofschulte. Harvey was the name of the first guy that Canaugh had arrested in his career with the Minneapolis cops years ago. He remembered it for that reason, and also because it was a fun name to say. Once he reached Santa Fe, Canaugh planned to stay in a hotel until he found an apartment. He planned to rent the apartment in the name of Harvey Hofschulte, though he had no identification for that name, and didn't plan to get any. He'd learned in his research that New Mexico was America's poorest state, and he figured that putting money on the table in most circumstances would permit him to do business the way he chose to do it. He wasn't planning on getting a New Mexico driver's license, even though state law expected him to obtain one within six months of becoming a resident. Regarding the license plates on his car, he figured that they might attract attention and so he planned to obtain New Mexico plates from a junked car. Having New Mexico plates and a New Mexico driver's license was critical only if his behavior caught the eye of the local cops. He figured that he could manage that. As a contingency plan, he still had his ID as a Minneapolis cop and his Minnesota private investigator license which he could produce if he needed to ask for leniency and he expected, rightly or wrongly, that the brotherhood (slowly becoming the sisterhood, too) of cops would understand.

Canaugh's money was all parked in the Cayman Islands.

Once he'd reached Miami in his earlier trip, he found a flight to the Cayman Islands. The Cayman Islands had the tightest bank secrecy laws in the world, surpassing Switzerland by the 1990's. There were almost 200 banks doing business in the Cayman Islands, most of them represented by modest offices in small office buildings. He chose National Westminster Bank because it was British. In the back of his mind, he thought that if he needed to flee the country he would be going to England. At this stage of his life, he wouldn't want to be learning any new languages. Opening an account for the Addison Clark Company was easy. The banker, a pleasant young woman happy to escape the gray chilliness of her native London, didn't even ask him what line of business the Addison Clark Company was in. If asked, Canaugh had decided in advance that he was going to say "financial reporting." Canaugh got instructions on wiring money into his new account, necessary because though he was now in his sixties, he'd never had to wire money before. He only spent one night in the Caymans, bothered by the expense of its food and lodging, and then flew back to Miami. He mentally thanked Thorpe for the idea of having a secret account in the Caymans.

Canaugh had chosen Santa Fe because the population was only around 30,000, about the same as St. Cloud, which he hoped would feel familiar. It had definite seasons in weather, like Minnesota, but nothing equivalent to the extreme cold and epic snowstorms that make Minnesotans occasionally cry out for mercy. There was good fishing nearby in the Pecos River. There was single-A baseball in Santa Fe and triple-A baseball in Albuquerque if he would ever need a night at a ballpark. If he ever felt that Santa Fe was too busy and wasn't safe enough for him, he could retreat to the nearby small towns of Taos or Pecos. Los Alamos was an hour away. Los Alamos was where the atom bomb had been developed during World War II. Most people there still worked as scientists for the federal government and secrecy was part of the town's culture.

When Canaugh reached Santa Fe, he was pleasantly

surprised that the city and the surrounding pine-covered mountains were even prettier than the pictures in the books he'd found at the library in St. Paul. He checked in for the first night at the New Santa Fe Trail Inn, a budget motel with a misleading name because it was far from new. He paid cash. When the clerk called him "Sir" he said, more for practice than anything else, "Call me Harvey." He ate at a Mexican restaurant that night, having developed some experience with Mexican restaurant menus by recent trips to La Cucaracha on Dale Street in St. Paul. He was unsure of the neighborhood he was staying in, so he moved all his belongings from his car into his motel room that night, mindful of the Albany nuns teaching Catholic schoolchildren that "It's a sin to create temptation."

He lay on his too-hard mattress in the dark, tired after two days of hard driving, but also enthused about having implemented his plan to deal with Thorpe. "Thank you, Doc," he said out loud to no one in the dark, picturing Doc's reddish face with the purplish lower lip hanging out. Canaugh had finally realized, while making his plans in the library, the meaning of Doc's admonition that "Your greatest strength and your greatest weakness are the same thing." To Thorpe, Canaugh's greatest weakness was that he was alone in the world without spouse or family, had limited assets, and was vulnerable to elimination without notice if Thorpe thought Canaugh might expose his plan. Thorpe's mistake was not realizing that, for the same reasons, Canaugh could disappear without a trace if he decided that Thorpe might be coming after him.

Canaugh knew that he could relax now that he was 1200 miles away from Minnesota. It was an unknown what the Crenshaws would do with his letter. If it got shared with Thorpe, no matter what the Crenshaws decided to do about Thorpe, surely Thorpe would have someone come looking for him, someone likely with instructions to do him great harm. Nothing was going to happen fast, Canaugh figured. He was going to be Harvey from Santa Fe for some time, maybe forever. At that moment, that outcome suited him just fine.

EPILOGUE

January 1995

Canaugh sat down in his apartment with the morning's copy of the Albuquerque Journal. As always, he pulled out the sports section first. Baseball news wasn't covered very extensively by the Journal in the off-season. A small story that morning about the Twins grabbed his attention. It said that Ira Thorpe, age 59, General Manager of the Minnesota Twins was retiring on short notice in advance of the annual winter meetings. Thorpe, according to the statement released by the Twins, felt that he had made a "solid contribution" to the success of the Twins but wanted to spend more time with his family. Leon Crenshaw would serve as acting General Manager while the team searched for candidates to replace Thorpe.

"Total bullshit," hooted Canaugh out loud. Fifty-nine-year-old well-paid big-league General Managers didn't suddenly give up their jobs to spend more time with their wives in quiet suburban homes. Reading between the lines, Canaugh decided that if the Crenshaws had solid proof they would have fired Thorpe. On the other hand, if they merely had lost faith in Thorpe after reading Canaugh's letter and doing any further research, they would have asked Thorpe for his resignation. Or perhaps, thought Canaugh, they really had the goods on Thorpe, but they still could have let him resign instead of firing him publicly. *Nah*, thought Canaugh, *that's not how the big boys react to a theft from their pile of money. If they had solid proof, they'd have canned him and told the world why*. The notion of "spending more time with family" language had become the bland and meaningless all-purpose reason when prominent people in the world of big business left their jobs. It was a phrase devised by public relations departments to obscure, rather than reveal, the actual truth.

Canaugh set down his paper and gazed at the pines on the mountains as the sun rose in the sky. He considered what this tiny article meant for his future. He had a jumble of thoughts. If there was any indication that Thorpe was being sent to prison, he could start planning on getting back to Minnesota. If the Crenshaws told Thorpe that it was Canaugh who'd revealed Thorpe's scheme, then some revenge act from Thorpe was likely. That made planning difficult. First of all, he'd never know what the Crenshaws told Thorpe and secondly, even if the Crenshaws never told Thorpe how they discovered his plan, Thorpe was astute enough to figure out that it was Canaugh that had fingered him. He had no way of knowing what was really going on back in Minneapolis. Canaugh was still at serious risk, even with Thorpe getting canned as the GM. Retribution from Thorpe was still highly possible. Only if Thorpe ever got prosecuted would Canaugh have some protection because if harm came to Canaugh under those circumstances, it would be obvious that Thorpe would have caused it. Canaugh's only option was to wait and see if anything happened to Thorpe.

Canaugh realized that he was left in limbo. "Limbo," snorted Canaugh as he remembered what the nuns had taught him as a boy about the meaning of the word. Limbo was a place, according to Catholic dogma, neither heaven nor hell, where unbaptized babies and the righteous who'd died before Jesus showed up on earth were sent. Canaugh remembered Ike telling him not to be righteous. Maybe Ike in his wisdom knew that the righteous either end up dead or in limbo. Canaugh realized now that his stay in Santa Fe wasn't going to end soon. Thorpe could have him killed. It wouldn't be too hard. There were so many poor people in New Mexico in need of cash. Santa Fe wasn't that far from Las Vegas, a one-hour hundred-dollar flight from the mob's hometown. Living as a recluse indefinitely had little appeal to Canaugh.

The next morning Canaugh was up early and dressed, with the apartment door half open. When he heard the footsteps coming, he stepped into the doorway and smiled. "Hi, I'm Harvey," he said to the woman who delivered his paper every day. "Care to go out for some coffee this morning when you're done with your job?"

The woman smiled. Her voice was warm and quiet, with a definite accent. She said her name was Pilar and that she could meet him at La Tortuga in one hour. Canaugh was not familiar with the name of the restaurant but looked up the address in the Yellow Pages. The place was some distance from the Plaza area where most tourists go for breakfast, but still within walking distance for Canaugh. La Tortuga was just a small brightly colored café, twenty feet wide at best. He was there fifteen minutes early. Sitting at the table, he realized that he was tense, concerned that she wouldn't show up and that his morning ritual exchange of smiles and nods with her could change, and even possibly end.

She appeared right on time and seemed familiar with the women who worked at the café. Canaugh let her do the talking and urged her to tell her life story, mainly so that he wouldn't have to share his own with her. He learned that she had come to the U.S from Mexico at age 12 in the back of a truck, speaking no English. She married at 18 and had two children, a girl who was a senior in high school and a son at New Mexico State in Las Cruces. "He's on the baseball team," she said proudly. Her husband had been killed ten years ago in a farming accident while working in Holtville, California. Although she delivered papers to help her children pay for college, she had a full-time job as a housekeeping supervisor at the Drury Hotel in Santa Fe.

"Two jobs—that's a lot for you," offered Canaugh.

She smiled patiently. "I have a third job. I'm a waitress here when they need some extra help. The owner is my aunt. That's why we moved to Santa Fe." Although she told Canaugh that she was due at the hotel by 10:00, they kept talking right up to the last possible moment when she had to leave. As she talked, Canaugh was charmed by her attractive face, her white teeth, and delicate lips. Most of all he liked the way she told her life story, one of considerable hardship and unending effort, without any trace of complaining. Canaugh wanted to find out if she had a boyfriend, so he asked if she'd ever remarried. "No," she said. "I've never found anyone. Found anyone who could compare to my late husband."

"I understand that feeling," said Canaugh, and the sympathetic look in her eyes told him that she instantly understood that he'd lost a spouse also.

"I'm happy though," she said. "I don't have much, but I've found that I can live on not much money."

Canaugh smiled a long time and finally, for reasons of his own, said, "That's good."

BOOKS BY THIS AUTHOR

A Little Pain

A Little Pain is a fictional account of a murder and a trial in the small Minnesota town of Plainview.

Shipmates: A Sea Story

SHIPMATES: A SEA STORY is a fictional tale of one sailor's life onboard a Navyship in the early 1970's.

Exemption: A Novel Of The Sixties

Exemption is a darkly comic tale about giving in to expediency.

Made in the USA
Columbia, SC
28 April 2023